Where Do You Go To, My Lovely?

Kim Evans

This is a work of fiction. Names, characters, places, and incidents are either products of the writer's imagination or used fictitiously.

Any resemblance to persons living or dead are purely coincidental.

Text copyright © 2023 by Kim Evans

All rights reserved

No part of this book may be reproduced or transmitted in any form or by any means, electronic, mechanical, photocopying, or otherwise, without expressed permission of the author.

ISBN: 9798863156293

Author Kim Evans

Editor Jodie Evans

Cover design by Kim Evans

For my dad x

Prologue

Nobody knows what I've done in the past and I'd like to keep it that way. If anyone found out, it would be the end for me and I don't think I'd do well in prison. So far nobody suspects me, I think I'm safe. Time to get out of bed and start a brand new day.

The lady we have to meet today is called Marie-Claire. I hope she's nice.

I smile at my reflection in the mirror and go to wake my partner.

"Let's go do this shall we?" I say.

1

Marie

I woke up earlier than usual this morning. I don't remember what I was dreaming about, but something startled me awake. I woke with a quickened heart rate and goosebumps spreading over my arms. I couldn't shake the weird feeling that made me jump out of bed so quickly, so I decided to leave my husband, John, in bed and head to the café on the corner of our quiet street in Blaengwynfi. I go to the café sometimes before the lunchtime rush to read in peace with a cup of tea.

The village is quieter than usual this morning. Birds are chirping from the rooftops of the terraced houses that line the street. This would drive John crazy, but at least they're not all black and lined up on the telephone wires, giving off a Hitchcock vibe like I've seen before. Although, that would be fitting with the eerie atmosphere here this morning.

As I take in my surroundings, I even begin to wonder if there's an eclipse today. It seems so dark for a late spring morning. The streets are empty, like everyone in the village is still asleep. Curtains are closed, bikes are abandoned in front gardens, and car windows are clouded with condensation. If one of those bike wheels starts to spin, I'll be preparing myself for Pennywise appearing from the lane halfway down the street. I suddenly feel a shiver creeping slowly through my skin, but it doesn't quite reach the surface.

It looks so different here on a bright summer's day with the sun's rays bouncing off the trees, creating a pattern of multiple shades of green that dance around as the wind gently blows them. The bird sounds are more like a chorus than the backing sounds for The Walking Dead on a day like that.

Today, every little sound like the whooshing of the trees blowing around and the creaking of a garden gate unsettles me, and I begin to pick up speed with every step.

When I finally step through the café door, my body releases that shiver that hid below my skin earlier, but it's one of warmth and relief. I feel less like a potential murder victim now.

I take a seat and Sophie, the barista, greets me with a warm, welcoming smile as she takes my order. She looks tired this morning. She can't conceal her yawns even though she tries to hide them by covering her mouth with her hand. Sophie took over the café a couple of years ago when her parents got too old to keep running it. Now that I've seen a friendly face and I'm surrounded by the smell of coffee brewing and the comforting heat from the log burner in the corner, I take my book out of my bag and let myself get lost in the world of Jane Eyre.

As I lower my book to take a sip of my tea, a man and woman I don't recognise enter the café. They're both wearing black suits. *A bit overdressed for the valleys* I think to myself, *probably trying to sell something.* They couldn't look more shady if they tried, especially the woman with her large dark sunglasses covering most of her face. In this weather, she just looks suspicious, like she's trying to disguise herself. I pick my book back up but can't help peering over the top of it to watch them.

They look in my direction and I divert my gaze back down to my book, trying to avoid making eye contact with these dodgy looking salespeople. I raise the book in front of my face and think *not me, not me, not me*, but they stroll over and take a seat right opposite me. I slowly lower my book and glance back and fore between the two of them, waiting for one of them to speak.

"Are you Marie-Claire?" the blonde lady with the big sunglasses asks me.

"Only my mother calls me that," I reply warily, "it's Marie."

The blonde lady has her hair slicked back into a low neat bun, with a very naturally pretty face, even with the stern expression. The guy looks about the same age as her, maybe late twenties or early thirties. His dark brown hair is neatly brushed back, but some strands are noticeably trying to break free.

They introduce themselves as Daniel and Sara, and tell me they're from a secret organisation called Collectors of the Past. I eye them both dubiously.

"Sorry, you're what?"

2

I regret missing the news on TV this morning and wonder if they mentioned anything about a crazy couple on the loose in South Wales. Before I have a chance to tell the two odd strangers sitting before me that I'm not interested in whatever they're selling, they continue to prattle on and I feel like a goldfish, opening and closing my mouth, trying to interrupt their nonsensical sales pitch. I've never wanted to shush someone so badly.

They tell me how they work for a secret agency that sends people back in time to collect items that no longer exist in the present, and how the items will all be stored somewhere for future references, along with other antiques that museums have no space for. The items vary, from toys to newspapers to decorative ornaments. Only one item can be collected per trip, so it takes several trips to collect every item.

They pause to gage my reaction after delivering their clearly well-rehearsed speech. I stare at them blankly, wondering what is going on here.

"I'm sure you have a lot of questions for us," Sara says. "Please feel free to ask us anything you want."

I only have about a hundred questions running through my head, mixed with a few mocking comments that I should probably keep to myself, but they've actually stunned me into silence.

They continue trying to convince me that this mission they have for me is real, so I nod along as though I'm listening intently, while trying to discretely look around for someone to come and save me from these idiots. If they knew what I was thinking right now, they'd probably leave the café deeply offended.

"You'd be paid very well, of course," Sara says, writing down a number on a piece of paper that makes my jaw drop. "And you can choose to go back to any time you want, as long as the item you need will be there on that day."

They tell me there are three specific items they need me to bring back. One is a beautiful tea caddy that my mam and dad kept in their display cabinet. I remember exactly what it looked like, black with gold edges and colourful Japanese style pictures around the sides. It was so ornate and elegant, and my mother loved it. Next is a teddy bear that I had as a child. I named it Amber because of its amazingly bright orange colour. It had a white mark just below one ear at the front, but I don't know how it got there. I think it was already there when I got it. The last item is a necklace that my dad had received as an heirloom from his grandmother.

I think about the smell of my mother's Sunday dinner cooking as my mind drifts off into our old kitchen. My mother watches over the pots on the stove, the windows are wide open to let the steam out. I swear I can smell it as I sit here in the café.

I think about what it would be like to be back there for real. I can't ignore the fact that these strangers know about three personal items from my past that really did exist, so after an hour of them trying to persuade me, I find myself getting curious. They're pretty convincing and the thought of revisiting my childhood makes my stomach flutter with excitement and nostalgia.

I think about the three items and when I would need to go back to. My parents had the tea caddy as far back as I can remember. I think it may have been a wedding gift so that would be there whatever day I choose to go back. I have no idea when my dad got his grandmother's necklace, but I suddenly have a very clear memory of the day I got Amber at a jumble sale. My mother was dressed up with make-up on and her long black hair flowing down her back, which was a rare sight. I remember that day so well because in the evening, I watched my parents dancing together in the garden as my dad serenaded her, and they looked happier than ever.

Daniel and Sara are staring at me now, waiting for me to respond to their almost unbelievable request.

"So, if I say yes, how exactly would I go back in time? How would I physically get there?"

As my mind begins to wander around images of giant mechanical time machines and DeLorean style cars, Daniel bursts my bubble by telling me it's a very simple, straightforward process.

"We'll give you a wristband, which you can input the date and place of where you'd like to travel to, then you close your eyes. When you open them, you'll be at your required destination."

I can't help but disappointedly blurt out, "A wristband? That's it?"

Daniel tries to hide a small laugh, but Sara remains serious and straight-faced.

No cool DeLorean for me then, I guess. Not a deal breaker but I expected something a little more exciting than a wristband.

We all order another hot drink as we discuss some more specific details. Sophie looks Sara and Daniel up and down suspiciously, then looks to me for reassurance that I don't need saving from the very out-of-place pair. It's an instinct for valleys residents to look out for each other, so I give Sophie the reassuring smile that she's searching for.

The tables around us have begun to fill with more of the village locals who send a friendly smile and good morning greeting my way, before curiously looking at Sara and Daniel, trying to work out who these strangers are. Some give me sympathetic looks, probably thinking I've been accosted by two pushy salespeople or religious representatives.

When I go to use the café toilets, as two cups of tea was too much for my bladder this early in the morning, I half expect Sara and Daniel to have disappeared when I return. Maybe they were just a figment of my imagination. I slowly peek my head around the door but no, they're still there, so I take a deep breath and make my way back to our table.

"So, what do you think?" Sara asks. "Are you interested?"

"Yes," I reply slowly. "I just need some time to think about it all and decide what dates I should go back to."

I ponder this for a moment and decide school days are definitely out. I never want to relive that hell again; I'd have to be dragged there kicking and screaming. The assemblies were the worst with all the hymn singing and watching the headmaster fall asleep on his chair. How rude is that? Even as a five-year-old that deeply offended me. None of us wanted to be singing hymns in the freezing cold school hall, but he could have made a little more of an effort, like I made the effort to mime so it looked like I was singing at least. It was probably better for everyone that way anyway, I could never carry a tune. John says it genuinely scares him when I sing. Sometimes that encourages me to sing more just to wind him up. He never looks impressed when I murder a Led Zeppelin song.

The only part of the school assembly that I actually didn't

mind was the walk there and back to the classroom as it passed some time without having to do any work. I can practically smell that school smell from the corridors as I reminisce. The snack and milk breaks were the only highlight of my days there. We used to have little glass bottles of milk with straws, but it's not worth going back in time just for that.

I think about all the old things I'd love to see again that have changed since I was a child, things that I love so much. Vintage telephones, jewellery, and, my favourite, the cars. Everything seemed so much classier back then, even though most families didn't have a lot of money.

"So, if you think you're up for it," Daniel says, interrupting my deep delve into childhood memories, "we can meet back here tomorrow? We'll bring the wristband and some paperwork that you'll need to sign."

It all sounds so weird when it's said aloud, but I nod along in agreement.

We say our goodbyes and I watch them leave. My head is spinning, I can't quite grasp what just happened. When they get outside, I notice that Daniel immediately moves closer to Sara as they walk, their fingers softly touching at their sides, like they want to hold hands, but they're trying to remain professional. I hope they don't wear the suits again when they come back tomorrow.

3

As I walk back to our three-bedroom terraced house, I wonder if John will even believe me when I tell him about my morning. I'm still not sure if I completely believe it myself, it sounds like something from a hidden camera show.

John and I are both out of work right now. John worked as a forklift driver until the company he worked for closed down recently. John grew up here in Blaengwynfi and I grew up a neighbouring village, so we've been settled here all our lives. There's something special about growing up in the valleys. You absorb it with every breath, it becomes a part of your soul. Even if you leave at some point, you know you'll be taking a piece of it with you.

As a child it was like living in an unexplored rainforest. We were constantly discovering new places, like a new footpath on the mountain or a new stream to bathe our feet in. Our list of favourite places to hang out was always growing. I'm intrigued to be reminded how it all used to look here, it's hard to picture it all sometimes knowing what it looks like now.

The mist begins to lift as I'm walking home. The sun has made an appearance and there are only a few clouds floating across the mountaintops. More people are out on the streets going about their daily business, some of them nod hello as they walk past, some call 'Good morning' from across the street. It feels like a regular morning again.

When I get inside, John is busying himself upstairs with sorting out some cupboards, which we've been meaning to do for weeks. I sit down on the bed and try to explain my very unusual morning to him, while checking for any signs that he might have set me up. He has an exceptional poker face so it can be hard to tell sometimes. One time, he tried to convince me that the hands of a clock take longer to go from six to twelve than twelve to six because of gravity. I didn't fall for that one, but I have been caught out a few more times than I'd like to admit, so John being behind this wouldn't surprise me at all. He can never resist an opportunity to wind me up. I usually manage to make a fool of myself on my own, but he likes to contribute when there's an opportunity. I try to reciprocate when I can.

John is a few years older than me, but he doesn't look it. He always keeps his hair short and neat, it suits him that way. At 5"10 he's quite a bit taller than me too. I barely scratch 5"3 and I've always been quite slim. On a windy day, I could probably blow over with a strong gust. We both have dark brown hair, mine is slightly darker. We've both gone through some hair transitions over the years, experimenting with different colours and styles. I'd love to be able to change my hair colour every day to suit my mood. Pink one day, then purple the next sounds like a dream.

It takes me twice as long to convince John than Sara and Daniel did to convince me, so I believe he doesn't know anything about it. He eventually gets curious, like I did, so he agrees I should find out more about it and even hints at trying to get him a trip back in time too. His favourite films are Back to the Future, so he's a little bummed too that there's no cool transport. He probably would have preferred something sportier and faster than the DeLorean though.

After we both voice our disappointment about the transport, I take a nice soak in the bath. I add some bath salts, light a few candles, and close the curtains to appreciate the full benefits of the candlelight. I can feel the tension lifting from my muscles as I lay there surrounded by soapy bubbles. I breathe in the aroma of the lavender and imagine all my aches being carried away with the rising steam. I think about the years that I'll need to go back to. Summer holidays would probably be my first pick. Christmas Day would be nice too.

4

The following morning, I make my way to the café again to meet Daniel and Sara. It's much brighter here this morning, which gives me more of a spring in my step as I quietly appreciate the less spooky atmosphere today.

When I reach the café, Daniel and Sara are already inside. They're dressed more casually today and I was clearly right about them being more than colleagues as I see them kiss across the table like nobody around them exists. He's holding her face in his hands like it's a pool of diamonds that he's trying to hold together so none of the sparkle escapes.

I hang on a minute longer outside, not wanting to disturb them. I think it's like learning a new language when you're getting to know someone romantically. If you're lucky, you'll become fluent, like John and I.

I eventually step inside, and they quickly untangle themselves from each other. They seem less business-like today though, so I have less of a compulsion to mock them in my head. I'm still struggling to believe it all though, even after being convinced yesterday.

We order some hot drinks and start discussing how everything works. They say I'm not allowed to discuss this with anyone else, apart from my husband. If he tells anyone, he'll be driven to quiet spot one day and used for target practice. Just kidding, that part isn't true. That's just a vision I had one day when I specifically asked him to do the dishes and they were still waiting for me two hours later. I imagined a funny version of the film *The Running Man*, where the contestants weren't killed, just slightly maimed and out of action for a day or two. The dishes would still be waiting for them when they'd recovered.

As Sara and Daniel continue to talk, I start to realise that this is actually going to happen, that I'll be going back to my childhood. My stomach does a little flip at the thought.

"You are permitted to bring one personal item back for yourself," Daniel says, "but only the one, so try to choose carefully."

I ask if I can go back to being two years old and bring back that energy for my next spring clean, but I already know the answer to that one and Sara looks like she doesn't appreciate the humour. We've all seen how quickly a two-year-old can destroy a room so imagine that in reverse.

"How about phones?" I ask. "Can I take my mobile or a camera, maybe get some photos to show John?"

"No, that's definitely not allowed," Sara replies firmly, but then her voice softens as she says, "I hope you'll be okay saying your dad again? Because it'll only be for a short time."

She's right, it won't be easy leaving each time. I'd say it'll be like losing him and missing him all over again, but that's never gone away.

I assure her I'll be fine. I know I'll be going to a time where I probably annoyed my parents endlessly, so I'll try to give them good days to enjoy by being on my best behaviour. Not every day though of course, it would look suspicious if I didn't act a little irrational as a child.

I tell them both I have one important request, more of a condition really.

"I want my husband to come with me one day, so that he can enjoy some memories with his mam and dad too."

Sara opens her mouth to respond but Daniel interrupts her, giving what I'm sure is a more friendly response than Sara would have given. "Unfortunately, that wouldn't be allowed, but you can give him the wristband to go back on his own, just for one day. You wouldn't both be able to go back together."

"That's great," I reply. "As long as he gets the chance to go back too, that's all that matters."

"We'll meet up in a few days to see how things are going, but you can contact us anytime if you have any questions," Sara says, and we exchange numbers.

Daniel tells me that once the items are collected and this job is done, they'll be taking a holiday together.

"It's been a while since we had a break," he says.

I tell them I'll try not to take too long, but I don't want to rush my time back either. They assure me they don't want me to do that, but I'm not sure I'm convinced Sara feels that way from the clearly forced smile she gives while saying it. Maybe she's just keen to get away, I can tell they're looking forward to it. They can't stop looking at each other and smiling every time they mention it. It's quite sweet.

I wonder if they have little competitions like me and John do. We have one where we try to lightly slap each other to see who has the best reactions, which isn't as bad as it sounds. It's just a gentle tap and the other one has to try dodge it. I would love to say I usually win but I don't, I lose pretty much every time. I have the reflexes of a sloth. John sometimes starts ducking and diving like a boxer in the ring, which he knows makes me laugh and throws me off even more. I either get fed up of losing and give up or we just end up laughing too much to carry on. I could recommend the game to Sara and Daniel, but that's our thing.

5

I spend the rest of the day trying to decide what date to go back to first. I'm thinking seven might be a good age to start with, I don't want to go too young. I want to be able to feed myself at least. I wonder if I did a better job of eating without making a mess at seven. I really can't imagine doing any worse than I do now. That's probably why John says takeaways at home are much more enjoyable than going out for a meal, I think he means less risky. I don't mind though because I prefer it too. I don't enjoy coming home after a meal out wearing half of it. At least I was at home that time I flipped a plate of beans on toast and it landed food side down in my lap.

It all seems so surreal now that I'm thinking about it more. I can't believe I get the chance to see my dad again. That's what made my decision so easy. I miss him so much; I could always talk to him about anything.

By the evening, I've decided on a Saturday in the summer of 1977. My stomach flutters with excitement, but I'm nervous too.

I curl up on the sofa with John in an attempt to try to relax myself and get an early night ready for my first trip back tomorrow. I tell John about my decision for tomorrow and that I'll probably want to leave quite early.

***

My alarm goes off at 7am. I'm too anxious to eat so I just have a quick cup of tea before I get ready. I realise that there's no point in getting dressed as I won't be wearing the same clothes when I get there anyway, or so I assume. We didn't really discuss anything like that now that I think about it. I guess I'll just have to be optimistic and hope for the best.

I leave John asleep in bed. I'll be leaving soon so it seems pointless waking him. I just write a little note for him, saying, "See you later babe xx."

I find myself rushing my tea, eager to get going. I don't want to over think the pros or cons anymore, so as soon as I finish, I wash my cup and head upstairs to set my wristband to the date, then close my eyes.

When I open them a second later, I'm lying in my old bed in my old pink bedroom, thankfully in my kiddie pyjamas.

At the bottom of the bed is the brown wardrobe that has just one door in the centre with a lock and key, and my white desk where I kept all my books. There's a line of toys laid out along the other side of the room. Among them is my old tree house, one of my favourite toys as a child. I'm surprised at how entertained it kept me. I spent most of the time transporting the figures up and down into the house, in the lift that you had to wind up and down. It was quite noisy, maybe that was the appeal to kids. Parents must have hated it. There wasn't really much else to it, just a few family figures, a dog, some bits of furniture, and a kennel outside for the dog. Amber, my bear, isn't here yet. I spot my old Snoopy watch on the desk, the first watch I ever had. It has a picture on the face of Snoopy laying on top of his kennel.

I hear movements downstairs and check the time. It's 8am,

so I guess I should get up. What kid sleeps in, right? I slowly walk around the room, running my fingers across my desk and taking in the sight of all my old possessions.

I emerge from the bedroom and creep slowly down the stairs, pausing to take a quick scan around the living room. Everything looks so retro now. It probably seemed so ordinary to me as a kid, but the room really is stunning. The brown patterned carpet, the old sofa with the plump multi-coloured cushions, and the small chunky TV with actual buttons on it. We had no remote controls then either, so I was the remote control. I'm going to get my exercise in today turning that thing over whenever a programme has finished.

I walk through the kitchen and there she is, my beautiful mother. She looks so young. She's wearing a blue skirt that sits just below her knees, and a patterned blue apron covering a white, short-sleeved top. Her hair is long and dark with just a hint of grey, probably helped along by yours truly. She always wore her hair tied back around the house. She looks happy making breakfast, singing along to the radio that's playing in the living room. I can't help but smile as I stand watching her. She looks up and sees me standing in the doorway.

"Hey, sleepyhead," she smiles. "Do you want some breakfast?"

"Yes, please," I reply. I request cornflakes because I remember how lovely they tasted covered with the cream from the top of the milk bottle. What a lovely treat to come back to. I take a seat and find myself swinging my legs under the dining table while I wait patiently for my breakfast. It really did taste better back then. I realise my feet aren't touching the floor from these chairs yet. The old wooden kitchen table was always covered with a tablecloth, apart from when my mother used it to roll out pastry. When she comes over to collect my empty dish, I touch her arm.

"Are my hands cold this morning?" I ask. I just wanted to touch her to make sure she's real.

She looks confused by the question but answers anyway.

"No, they feel fine," she replies. "Do you want to go wimberry picking later? I can make a tart for tomorrow teatime."

"If I'm good, can I have a piece later?" I ask, knowing I won't be here tomorrow.

"We'll see," she says. When parents say 'we'll see', kids always hear 'yes'. That hasn't changed, I'm already looking forward to my piece of wimberry tart later on.

After I've devoured my cornflakes, Mam tells me she's put my clothes out on my bed ready for after my wash. I go back upstairs to the bathroom, very aware that my dad is still in bed in the next room. I have a quick wash in our old minimalistic bathroom, with just a bar of soap on the sink and a couple of towels on the rail.

My mother has put out one of my dresses that I probably loved at the time but not so much now. It's a pink corduroy one, with dungaree-style straps. There's a white, long-sleeved top to go underneath. I'm not sure why I liked this dress at all, it's so stiff and uncomfortable. Not the best outfit to play in or climb mountains picking wimberries. Still, it's a small price to pay for coming back. I don't want to waste any time arguing about clothes this morning. A child rarely wins an argument with an adult anyway. No matter how hard we try, we always end up sounding like the unreasonable ones.

I remember that having my hair brushed is next, so I stall and hang around the bedroom looking at some of my toys. I have a pile of books, Lego, and my Sindy dolls and furniture sets. I forgot that I had so many of them. This must have been after my Tiny Tears phase.

When I leave the bedroom, I linger around my parent's bedroom door. I just want to see my dad. I creep into the bedroom to see if he's awake yet or if I can get a glimpse of him asleep in their dressing table mirror. He's still asleep but he stirs when I walk in.

"Hey, what time is it?" he asks groggily. "Everything okay?"

I'm frozen to the spot for a moment. My dad is really here.

"Everything's fine," I say, when I can finally speak again. "I think it's about nine o'clock. I'm going wimberry picking with Mam later. Will you be up before we go?"

He says he'll be up soon. I leave the bedroom, slide down against the door onto the floor, and try not to let any tears escape because I know I have to go back downstairs. I have to compose myself and remember to act like a seven-year-old.

I have a feeling the tears will flow pretty soon anyway though when I see my mother sitting on the sofa, hairbrush in hand. Did parents have to be so brutal with it? I know I brushed my hair before I left this morning, so there couldn't possibly have been that many knots. Once the torment of that is finally over and I feel like I've had a garden rake run over my head about a hundred times, I ask if I can wear braids to bed from now on. I wonder why I didn't think of that when I was a child. No knots in the morning.

6

Daniel

"I don't feel good about misleading Marie. She seems like a really nice person."

Sara rolls her eyes and tuts softly but tries to play it off as playful when I frown at her response.

"She'll be fine, she won't know what she's bringing back for us," she says. "Don't make such a big deal about it."

She leans her elbows on the kitchen counter in our temporary flat in Swansea, provided for us while we work on this job.

"Can't we just be honest and tell her? Then we can let her decide for herself if she still wants to be involved."

"No, Daniel, you know we can't risk it. How do you see that conversation going? Excuse me but if you could bring back something that will help create a virus that could kill millions of people that would be great. Not to mention what our boss would do to us if we told her."

"But it's to create a strain to find a cure or treatment in case it's needed in the future. It could save a lot of people," I reply.

"We know that, but she probably wouldn't believe it. And the virus has to be made first, I told you that. It's just better that she doesn't know anything, okay?"

"How do they even know Marie had the bear?" I ask.

"There was a school photo in a newspaper that showed Marie holding the bear and it was unique in some way apparently. Something to do with a mark below one of the ears. She has no idea what she had. It got lost years ago when some woman was supposed to hand it over but she never showed up. No one knew where it was until that photo of Marie was in the paper. That's what Liam says anyway."

"It must have been sold on in a shop or something," I suggest.

Sara can be a worrier at times, but she tries to hide it. I try to reassure her as much as I can, though.

"Marie seems a bit ditsy anyway. I doubt she would even understand or care," she says.

"That's a bit unfair, she's just different to you. I bet she's smarter than you think."

"I'm not saying I dislike her," Sara replies defensively. "She seems okay, maybe a bit guarded. I just don't think she would care about any of this. She's looking forward to going back to her past so can't we just let her enjoy it? She really doesn't need to know."

I can't help but get the feeling that she's trying to convince herself more than me now.

"When you put it that way, I suppose it does make sense. And wouldn't you feel guarded being practically pounced upon by two complete strangers with a story that, let's be honest, sounds ridiculous."

She shrugs. "Don't forget, when this is over we'll probably never even see Marie again, so there's no need to get too invested in how this affects her."

Another callous comment from her that I try to ignore. She does have a bit of an edge to her sometimes that I think would be wrong to cross, but I always give her the benefit of the doubt because she is truly lovely most of the time, especially to me. I try to search her face for clues sometimes about what she's thinking but she's good at keeping herself hidden away.

7

Marie

Dad comes downstairs looking as cheerful as he always did. He always had such a pleasant look about him, and I remember my lovely grandfather being the same. I've never forgotten an inch of his face, but I still can't help staring at him when he isn't looking at me.

I ask if he'd like to play a game of monopoly with me before I go wimberry picking. I want to spend some quality time with him while I'm here. He brings his coffee over to the table and gets the board out of the cupboard. He hands me the dog because he knows that's what I always choose to play with.

After a while, Mam comes in from the kitchen, which everyone called the back kitchen then. I never got why that was, that one always puzzled both me and John.

"We'll have to get ready in a minute now to go wimberry picking," she says.

Dad says we can leave the monopoly board out to finish our game later.

"Mary and Lisa are coming with us," Mam yells from the kitchen while she collects some tubs for the wimberries. Mary and Lisa are our neighbours. Lisa is the same age as me and she's incredibly annoying. From what I remember, she always tried to get me in trouble by complaining about everything I did and often made up lies about me, which I hated her for. I hope my bad memories are exaggerated, but they're not.

While we're out, Lisa complains endlessly and tells my mother that I flicked her ear three times when she wasn't looking. She's lying, it was just the one time. I couldn't resist, she was being such a brat. She watched as I collected my wimberries, then grabbed two handfuls of mine and put them in her tub. I was so proud of how much I'd collected. I just want to push her head into her tub and give her a purple face wash, but I don't. I'm also proud of myself for that, because it takes a lot of restraint.

I think my mother knew that sometimes Lisa tried to get me in trouble so I'm not too worried about still getting a slice of wimberry tart later.

Lisa aside, our day picking wimberries was more fun than I had expected. I'd forgotten how much I used to enjoy this, spending the day out in the fresh air, with a refreshing walk around the beautiful mountains looking for the fullest wimberry bushes. This is just what I needed today. It's stunning here in the summertime, with all the different trees randomly spread around us and the bright flowers in the fields making patterns like a kaleidoscope. I couldn't think of a better view I'd like to be looking at right now.

Mary asks if I'd like to go back to theirs for tea. I think the no came out of my mouth before she'd even finished her sentence. I didn't want to seem rude though, so I said, "I just want to finish my game of monopoly with my dad when we get back." What I really wanted to say was, "I don't want to spend a minute longer with Lisa than I have to, she's an annoying little shit." I just have the urge to flip her the bird every time she looks at me. Instead, I stick my tongue out at her, which doesn't have the same satisfying feeling at all, but it will have to do. This trying to act my age is hard.

"That's okay, you can come over tomorrow instead," Mary says.

"I suppose," I reply, dragging my feet and dropping my arms like an orangutan. I suddenly feel bad for seven-year-old me tomorrow. As a parting gift, Lisa gives me a little shove near a bunch of stingy nettles, leaving my knees covered in stings. This means I'll get covered with vinegar by my mam when I get home and smell like the local chippy. If there's no vinegar, my knees will be buttered like a slice of bread. The joys of being a child in the seventies.

Dad is watching one of his favourite western films when we get back, so Mam asks if I'd like to help in the kitchen while I'm waiting. I used to love watching her bake, so I sit at the table while she prepares pastry for the tart and gets the ingredients ready to make a sponge cake. First though, she douses me in vinegar. I was hoping she'd forget about that.

After playing with the leftover bits of pastry on the table while Mam mixes the ingredients for the sponge in her big mixing bowl, she asks if I'd like to lick the bowl or the spoon. I would have loved this at seven, but at forty-eight I'm thinking *do I really want salmonella tomorrow?* I think not. So, probably for the first time ever, I decline the offer. Getting my hands messy with pastry dough and flour is surprisingly invigorating though.

After closely dodging salmonella, I finish my monopoly game with my dad which I win, but I know he always lets me win. I've decided to take the tea caddy back with me today. I ask Mam if I can borrow it to take upstairs to put some of my pencils in. I promise to be careful and immediately feel bad for doing so.

Of course I'll have to say I broke it so I hide it under the bed, ball up some newspaper to pretend that's where all the smashed bits are, and put it in the bin. My mam takes it surprisingly well when I tell her. I think she's just too tired to scold me tonight. I kind of wish she had though, then maybe I wouldn't feel so guilty. I know how much she loved it. She still cuts me a piece of tart, pours some warm custard over it, and tells me it doesn't matter.

"Accidents happen," she says.

The tart tastes lovely, flavour bursting from the wimberries like little sparks of electricity striking my tongue.

8

As I sat enjoying my dessert that evening, I wondered how much time both my mam and dad spent worrying about me and how my life would turn out. I'd love to be able to tell them that I'm very happy in the future. I'm married to my soulmate and our children are all grown up and have begun families of their own. Not having to worry about me every day would be a great gift to give them, but I know I can't do that. They wouldn't believe me anyway.

I make my way up to bed knowing I'll be back again soon. I leave my parents in peace to watch the evening shows that they like, collect the tea caddy from under the bed, and take another look around my bedroom. As much as I've loved being back here, I have missed John today. Being in a different decade makes me feel like I'm a million miles away from him. It's an unsettling feeling.

When I get back, John is playing fetch in the living room with Chewy our chihuahua. He likes to run around for an hour playing every evening before bedtime. Chewy that is, not John.

I tell John about how my day went while he pours me a cup of tea. I tell him how great it was to see my dad, and that I was surprised how young my parents looked. Also how unpleasant it was spending time with Lisa. I forgot how annoying kids could be at seven. I was no angel, but it seemed like it was her life's mission to make me miserable back then. Her family moved away when I was about twelve and I never saw her again. I remember the day they left, I could barely contain my excitement. I remember thinking that a street party wouldn't have been totally inappropriate.

We chat for a while about all the old furniture our parents used to have, and how different the decor was. You forget about so many of the little things that used to be around until you actually see them again.

I send Sara a text to ask if we can meet tomorrow so I can give her the tea caddy. She seems surprised that I got it so quickly and she's keen to meet up.

I have a good look at it and show it to John before I have to part with it tomorrow. I always loved looking at it in the display cabinet, it stood out among all the other ornaments in there.

We head on up to bed once Chewy has settled down and I look for a film for us to watch, which we will probably fall asleep to. We put one on every night, sometimes taking longer to choose a film than we do actually watching it. Tonight is no exception, I'm sleeping within ten minutes of getting into bed.

***

The morning seems to arrive in a blink. I don't want to get up right away, I feel exhausted after yesterday. My muscles feel like they don't work when I try to move. I'm regretting asking Sara to meet today now, I had no idea I would feel like this. I wonder if there's a flu going around but when I ring Sara to explain and tell her I'll have to arrange to meet up another time instead, she tells me it's a side effect of the time travel. She could have mentioned that before, at least I would have been expecting it then. The tea caddy isn't going anywhere anyway, so there's no rush.

There's a lot of sighing coming from Sara, like she's annoyed, and she asks if there's anything else wrong.

"Apart from feeling like a used punch bag, I'm fine thanks," I can't help remarking. She sounds a bit impatient for someone who says I have as much time as I like to get these things back from the past. I just put the phone down and go back to sleep for a while.

9

Daniel

Sara storms into the kitchen, sighing loudly with her phone in her hand.

"Marie just cancelled on us," she tells me, putting a hand on her hip.

"She's probably exhausted after yesterday," I say reassuringly. "We forgot to tell her how tired it would make her feel actually. Being seven one day and doing anything you want with all that energy and then going back to being forty-eight, it can be hard on the body. You know that, it was in the information we had." I try to reassure her by stroking her arm supportively as she sits down on the stool opposite me.

"Yes, I told her that on the phone. She didn't sound happy that we forgot to mention it. She seemed so keen to meet up last night. I need to encourage her to bring the teddy bear back next, just in case." She shrugs me off, stands up abruptly and starts pacing around.

"I wouldn't pressure her too much. She's only been back once, give her a chance. And wouldn't you be upset too? That's kind of an important bit of information we left out."

"What if she discovers there's something inside the bear when she gets it? What do you think she would do?" Her eyes begin to widen with panic as she's clearly going through every worst-case scenario in her head.

"She's not going to find it, it's sewn inside. Don't worry so much," I tell her.

She stares at me for a minute, like she wants to believe me but she's unconvinced.

"If you say so," she says finally, "but I think we should keep a closer eye on her."

I ask her to come and sit back down but she ignores me.

"Look, there's no need to start getting paranoid." As she paces past me, I gently pull her onto my lap and she caves, cracking a smile and looping her arms around my neck. "Look, let's just have a nice day together. There's not a lot of work we can do at the minute anyway while we're waiting for Marie to get all the items. We could go out for food or go to the beach? I'll treat you to ice cream," I say with a smile.

Sara always seems to be in a panic about something lately. If she spoke to me about what was bothering her, maybe I could help. She seems nervous around Liam sometimes too, I don't know why. I've only met the guy once but he seemed nice enough.

"Okay," she replies. "We could go out I suppose, just for a little while. Maybe it'll take my mind off things a bit." She pauses, looking at me intently. "You know I love you right? I just get frustrated sometimes with work, and I know you like Liam, but I find him a bit intimidating, so be careful, okay?" she says.

Her comments leave me wondering if there's something going on with this job that I don't know about.

She stands up and continues to move uneasily around the flat as she tidies up before we get ready to head out. I thought I'd made her feel better but she still seems fidgety and on edge, like she can't relax. I watch her check her reflection in the mirror and notice she looks disappointed with herself. When I look at her, I can't believe how lucky I am. We met at college and became good friends. After college, we went in different directions for a while but then reconnected last year and became inseparable. We just randomly bumped into each other one day on the street and it felt like it was meant to be.

I know that she doesn't want to have to work again after this and, I must admit, it would be nice to do whatever we want all day instead of doing this.

We could even think about starting a family, although this hasn't been discussed yet. Sara doesn't talk about children much, but I think she would make a terrific mother. I know I'll do my best to be a good dad. We have talked about getting married someday. Sara wants to get married somewhere exotic, just the two of us, which is absolutely fine by me. It's just the way I would have chosen to do it anyway.

When Marie was telling us about her husband John, she mentioned that they got married without telling anyone. She always has this shine about her when she talks about John. It was just the two of them in their local registry office. They couldn't afford anywhere exotic. Maybe they could use some of the money to book a nice holiday. I think exotic to them would be somewhere in North Wales instead of South, but it sounds like they're happy wherever they are. Wales is a beautiful place anyway. I suddenly realise that I'm going to miss it when we move on.

10

Marie

It's 9.30am when I wake again, but I still feel exhausted, like all the energy has been drained out of my body. I can't believe Sara and Daniel didn't tell me about this. I turn from one side onto the other to check if the muscle aches have eased. They feel slightly better than they did earlier.

I think about yesterday and how quickly the day went by. I barely had a chance to absorb any of it, but every memory of it makes me smile today. Yes, even my time with Lisa. I am still a bit miffed about the stolen wimberries though.

I go into the bathroom to brush my hair and find that even that is an effort today. I compare my long dark hair to my mams from back then. I have a little more grey in mine, but I usually keep it tied back most days, like she did. I don't look as tired as I expected to this morning, considering how I feel.

John must have heard me getting up because when I go downstairs, he has a cup of tea and some biscuits ready for me.

"I feel so tired, I just want to relax today," I tell him.

"That's fine by me. We can just sit outside in the sun for a while this afternoon if it stays warm enough," he says.

We both like the serene lifestyle that comes with living in a small village. The views around us are amazing to look at. What more could we ask for?

I think about the money we'll get paid at the end of this. It'll buy us anything we need, which isn't much really. John will want a new car no doubt, and I'd like to buy a house, maybe the one that we currently rent. The rest will just be used for keeping us and our family comfortable.

"Will you come with me to meet Sara and Daniel next time?" I ask John, as we sit on our chairs in the front yard after lunch. "Sara was doing my head in with her pushy attitude on the phone this morning."

"Yes, if you want," he says. "Maybe I can ask them a few questions myself. But you can refuse to go back anytime you want if you don't feel happy with anything."

"I'll be fine, I'd just like the company. Plus, you should meet them, see what you think about them."

"The crazy suit people? Can't wait."

"They've ditched the suits. I think it was pretty clear to them that they were drawing attention to themselves. It was funny though." We both have a laugh about it.

I pop back inside to get a hat as the sun is already burning into my head. It's going to be hotter than we expected today, with only a subtle suggestion of a breeze.

"I was worried that something might go wrong yesterday and that you wouldn't be able to get back," John admits with a sigh, like it's a relief to say. "I'll probably worry again next time you go too."

I reach over and take his hand.

"It was strange not having you there," I say. It felt like he was so far out of reach, like I was in a completely different world. I suppose I was, in a way. I felt homesick for my present life. When I tell John about the wimberries incident with Lisa, he jokes that I should get over it as it was forty-one years ago now. How can you argue with that?

When we step back inside, our eyes trying to readjust from the sunlight, I feel like my sweat glands have had a new burst of energy. I feel hotter now than I did outside. I'll take a shower when I've cooled down a little.

While I'm waiting, I think about my next trip back. At least I'll have an idea of what to expect next time. I'll try maybe age eight or nine, and it will definitely be a Sunday. I have to have one of my mother's roast dinners and Sunday desserts. I'd say I wish I knew what ones she made on certain dates, but I know it would take me forever to decide then. There were so many that I liked, and John says I'm one of the most indecisive people he's ever met. I know he's not wrong about that.

As my mind is on food, I remember one of my favourite sandwiches that I used to make on a Sunday evening. We always had a second helping of some potatoes, meat, a little bit of veg, and gravy that was leftover. I used to make a sandwich of half potatoes and half sprouts. The sprouts in bread and butter was just delicious. Any time I've told someone this, I could tell I was being silently judged. I think I take after my dad where food is concerned. He used to eat beef dripping sandwiches, which sounds disgusting, but all the men in the village used to eat them. Cabbage water was another of mine and my dad's favourite things on a Sunday while waiting for dinner. Yes, I know that sounds bad too and I think I will have to pass on that one. Some things don't age like a fine wine.

That evening, we get some old photos out of the cupboard to look at. We try to get some ideas of how different things looked over the years. Some of the snow ones are surprising to look at now, we had quite a few bad blizzards back then. It must have taken weeks for the snow to melt away. There's no denying how lovely it all looked in the snow though. We hadn't even noticed how quick the time has gone this evening. The rest of the photos will have to wait for another time.

I decide to get the necklace next time I go back and leave the teddy bear until last.

***

As I slip into bed tonight my mind is all over the place, like a disorganised filing cabinet. I loved seeing my parents and being back in my old home, but what if something did go wrong and I couldn't get back here? I don't really want to consider that as a possibility. I can't even picture my life without John, so I try to block that thought out.

Maybe I'll go back sooner rather than later. It feels like a tornado is doing laps around my thoughts, blocking the view so I can't see them clearly. I'm too tired to even try making sense of anything anymore tonight. I drift off into an unsettled sleep.

When I wake up in the morning after a restless night, I tell John that I'm going to go back again today.

"I want to do it all as soon as possible, so I can get back to normal. As much as I loved going back, I just don't feel as comfortable doing this as I thought I would." I lean my head against John, it relaxes me.

"Okay, just enjoy your time there with your parents and try not to think about anything else," he says.

"You're right, that's all I need to focus on. It was lovely seeing how different everything was back then, there's so much you forget about. You have to visit a shop when you go back. I'd forgotten how many different sweets were around back then. Do you remember Spangles?"

"Yes, and the Hubba Bubba bubblegum," he says.

There were always loads of different jars of sweets to get a quarter of. Me and my dad would both choose a different one and share them later so we would have two sorts each.

"Are you looking forward to your day back?" I ask.

"Yes, I can't wait to see my mother and father."

"Don't forget though, you're not really a child so no tormenting your sister."

"Don't ruin my fun," he replies. I know my words are wasted, he won't be able to resist. What is it with older siblings having to constantly harass the younger ones?

I'm going to ask Sara if John can go back next time. I don't want them backing out and disappointing him. He seems to be really looking forward to it now. Me on the other hand, I'm feeling more like a concerned parent instead of a wife. He's told me about all the falls he had on his bike. I'm hoping he'll come back in one piece, not battered and bruised.

As kids, we never seemed to fear anything, and didn't see the dangers we do now. No wonder we had so much fun. I think we don't worry as children because our parents did all the worrying for us, then when we have children of our own it becomes our time to worry. At least his mother will be there to fix him up before he gets back if he does fall. They always had a knack for making us feel better. I would probably just yell at him for being so stupid at his age. I think I'll need a few distractions that day.

11

Sara

I wonder sometimes about Daniel. He seems to question me a lot lately about our work, it's unnerving. I feel like I'm going to let something slip. I need to try to keep him distracted. The less he knows about the truth the better, but I'm struggling to keep up this pretence every day. I wish Liam had just told me as much as he told Daniel. I think he did it on purpose to keep me in line, and for me to keep Daniel in line. He knows I'm desperate to get my hands on some easy money, and that I'm not really concerned about how I get it.

My mind keeps going back to last year when one of our clients, Tina, had an accident. It was after questioning our motives for sending her back in time. There were several items Liam needed, and the woman was holding out on the last one.

She fell over a balcony, but the police said the circumstances were suspicious. I can't help but suspect Liam was responsible for her death. Every time I brought it up, I would get dismissive comments like, "She probably got what she deserved," or "That's what happens when you stick your nose in where it's not wanted." He never denied being involved and I know he's capable of something like that, or at least capable of ordering it to be done. Tina didn't seem the type to back down from anything, but she wouldn't have stood a chance against Liam's men. I try not to show Liam how uneasy I am around him, but I can't help it sometimes. You can feel his stare burning into you even if you're not looking at him.

"I'll text Marie this evening to see if she'll meet up soon for an update," I tell Daniel.

"Okay. I wonder if she's enjoying her time in the past with her parents," he says.

"Why do you even care?" I snap back.

Daniel gives me a surprised, wounded look.

"Sorry, I'm a bit tired today and I just can't wait until this job is over and we can take a break."

"Not much longer now," Daniel says. 'Then it'll be just the two of us for two weeks in the sun."

Maybe I'll just tell him the truth when this is all over and hope that he'll be able to trust me again somehow. He thinks Liam wants the virus to help to discover a treatment or cure, not to sell it to the highest bidder.

Liam says we need people like Daniel, people who are easy-going and pleasant, to make the clients trust us. I probably should have felt insulted by that but who am I kidding, all I wanted was a nice pay cheque at the end of this and Liam knew it. I'll be happy once I've got my money, but I can't help feeling bad sometimes about being dishonest with Daniel.

"I'll text Marie tomorrow. We can order a takeaway and watch a film this evening. Does that sound good to you?"

"That sounds great," he replies.

That does sound good but what I really need is for all of this to be over and to be sitting on a beach somewhere in the sun with a full bank account, but I don't say that out loud.

12

Daniel

I told Sara that I'm nipping to town today to get some groceries, but the truth is I'm going to visit my dad. I've not told Sara much about him yet, I don't want her to know he's an alcoholic. She doesn't know I still have any contact with him, she thinks we're estranged, and when she pushed for more information, I insisted I didn't want to talk about it. I love my father and I'm not ashamed of him, I just don't want Sara asking too many questions about my mother or how she died. My mother was an embarrassment. She slept around, was always drunk, and the way she started dressing made me sick, I couldn't even look at her. That led to my dad's drinking and that's why I had to get rid of her, before she drove him into an early grave. My dad doesn't know, he thinks it was an accident and I want to keep it that way. He's been better off without her. He's fallen off the wagon now, it happens sometimes, but I always help him get back on his feet again. He wouldn't even try to stop when she was still around. I don't mind helping him. I love my dad, he's been through a lot.

Sara already has enough on her plate anyway with this job.

I can tell she worries about me too which is just like Sara. She can be so sweet, unlike my ex-girlfriend, Helen, who started out nice then started to change. She had to be dealt with; I couldn't let her treat me or any other man that way. That won't happen with Sara. I know it won't. She would never lie to me or disrespect me. Every time I think of her it makes me smile. She's special.

Besides, I've followed her a few times when she says she's going to work to see Liam and when she says she's going shopping, and that's exactly what she does, so I know she doesn't lie to me.

One time, I followed her shopping and sat in a café across the street. I could see her through the windows coming out of the changing rooms to stand in front of the full-length mirror. She looked so radiant and happy, twirling around and smiling to herself. It felt like I was seeing her for the first time again. She was blissfully unaware that anyone was watching. It was like at that moment she didn't have a care in the world, she was just a young girl in a shop playing dress up.

I let myself into my dad's flat with the spare key he gave me years ago. The curtains are all closed, he must still be in bed. I open them to let some light in and put the kettle on.

"Dad?" I call.

"I'll be out now, son," he calls back gruffly.

"Okay, I'll put the kettle on."

I pick up the empty snack wrappers and cans littered around on the floor. At least I know he's eating something, I suppose, even if it is junk.

He stumbles into the room, rubbing his tired, puffy eyes when the light hits them. He stands in the doorway, looking around at the now tidier room, and then looks at me.

"Sit down, Dad," I tell him. "I'll get you a cup of coffee and then make some breakfast."

"I'm sorry, son," he says. "I just keep letting you down."

"I don't want to hear that Dad, you could never let me down. I'll look out for you, I always have. I'm sorry Mum gave you such a hard time and did this to you."

He can never look me in the eye when I mention her. He knows deep down that this is all her fault, but he'll never admit it.

"Don't blame her Dan, you know I don't like to talk about it."

"I don't know how you can still defend her after all this time," I say, "but okay, I won't say any more about it. Just promise me you'll eat your breakfast and go to a meeting today."

"Deal," he says, holding out a shaky hand so we can shake on it. "I'll be okay, don't worry about me."

I grab the bag of groceries I bought on the way and stock his fridge and cupboards.

"Right, let's get this breakfast going. I think I'll join you actually."

"You seem happy," Dad says. "Things going well with that new girlfriend you've been seeing?"

"Sara," I reply. "Yes, things are great, I think she's the one." I can't help smiling as I say that.

"Steady on now, Daniel. You thought Helen was the one, but then she left, and you never saw her again."

No one will ever see her again.

"It's different this time, really. Sara is smart, stunningly beautiful, and she's the most honest person you'll ever meet. I can't believe how lucky I am. I'll bring her to meet you one day when work is less hectic."

I can't stop long at Dad's today, but I'll come back again in a day or two to check on him. I don't want to leave Sara alone too long, she seems so stressed with work at the moment. I need to keep an eye on her.

13

Marie

I'm feeling a bit better this morning about going back again. I've decided on a Sunday during the summer of 1978.

John goes downstairs to make tea while I take a shower. I'm not really a breakfast person, not since I was a kid anyway.

When I go downstairs after my shower, I sit with John to ask what his plans for the day are. Chewy is still asleep under his blanket, making the faintest snoring sounds.

"You're so lucky you get to have a nice freshly cooked roast dinner today," John says. "Remember those thick fluffy Yorkshire puddings our mothers used to make?" He's almost drooling, but I understand. I wish I could bring a few of those back with me and freeze them for the next few weeks. And as someone who always checks best before dates, I think I could overlook the fact that they would be forty-one years old. Our mothers made the best Yorkshire puddings, cooked in a round baking tin like a sponge cake, and cut into slices to share out.

"I'll have to watch my mother make it today and pick up some tips. There always seems to be something missing when

I try to make it."

"Talent?" John replies. He's lucky I know he's joking.

"And when I get it right, there won't be any for you," I joke. "I'd better head off. It's funny, I just automatically assume I have to leave in the bedroom to arrive in my old bedroom, even though we're not even in the same house. Am I just being weird?"

"Are you ever not?" John says with a smile.

"Good point." John always makes me laugh. I love that I can be a little ditsy around him and it doesn't bother him at all, never has.

I still go up to the bedroom to leave.

***

I arrive in 1978, in bed again. I wonder if I was a lazy child or if we didn't get up so early without computer games to play or a lot of choice of what to watch on TV. I can't remember what time the TV programmes started in the mornings, but I know there were none throughout the nights like there are now. Programmes would finish around midnight every night.

When I get up for breakfast this time, everything feels more familiar and comfortable. I ask for a dish of shredded wheat, my favourite cereal when I was a kid, with that lovely creamy milk again.

My dad walks into the kitchen and says he'll take me for a walk to see the horses when I get dressed after breakfast. There were a few in a field we used to visit on a farm just down the road.

This is just perfect. I had a day out with my mam last time and now I get an hour or so out with my dad. I go and get dressed. It gives Mam some space to start preparing the Sunday roast in peace and I can help with the vegetables when I get back, something I used to enjoy doing.

The village is very quiet on Sunday mornings, but not the eerie type of quiet, the peaceful kind, like the village is resting today. Most shops didn't open on a Sunday back then, and if they did, it was just for an hour or two in the morning. We pop into one that's open and get some sweets for later. I choose a packet of fruit bonbons, an old favourite of mine. I'll share them with my dad later, and he'll share the sherbet lemons that he bought with me. Mam isn't much of a sweets person. She'll keep one or two in her apron pockets and maybe treat herself once in a while, but she usually ends up giving them to me. I'll slip a couple of bonbons in her pocket later though because I know she likes the red ones.

We spend half an hour or so feeding and stroking the horses. I'm usually quite nervous around them now but I didn't seem to have that fear of them as a kid. There are three here, each their own unique colour: one is chocolate brown, one is beige with a white patch on his chest, and one is jet black. They're all equally stunning to look at. They take the hay from our hands quite gently, so that it tickles my palm. I enjoy the familiar walk down the lanes with fields all around us, some with cows and some with sheep. It was a popular place for family walks. Even when there were lots of people here at the same time, it still felt like such a tranquil place to be. This morning there are just a couple of dads out walking with their children, all of the mothers are at home preparing dinner. I enjoyed these walks with my dad. I believe that he still watches over me in the present time, how could he not? He's been doing it all my life. On the way back home, we encounter Lisa and a few other kids from the street playing on the pavement.

"Come and play with us," she calls to me. My dad encourages me to stay for a bit and play with them. Good going dad, this is going to be a nightmare. Despite how great it is to see him again, I can't hide the frown I'm now displaying.

I'm roped into a game of hopscotch and, to my surprise, end up actually enjoying it. It's not every day you get to play like a child again, it's exhilarating. I have forgotten the rules though, which angers Lisa, who complains that I'm doing it wrong on purpose to make my turn last longer. She's not entirely wrong. She gets to play it tomorrow and I don't so I'm going to make the most of it. It almost ends when Lisa says, "I'm not playing anymore and I'm taking my chalk home with me". I'd forgotten how childish kids could be, I want to tell her to grow up. Instead, I talk her into staying out a bit longer by promising to be nicer to her, which makes me cringe to say but I'm just thinking about how it'll affect the younger me tomorrow. Lisa could pout for days.

I remember one of my favourite old TV shows, *Bewitched*, and try to wiggle my nose like Samantha to see if, when Lisa throws her hopscotch stone, it'll just fall on number one. I used to try that often when I was younger. It never worked but it was always fun to pretend that it would.

When I've tolerated her and Ben, the nose-picker from up the street who joined our game, for as long as I possibly can, I go in to help my mam with the vegetables.

By now there's not much left to do except pop some peas from the pods, which was one of my favourite things to help with. We would sit on the sofa with a bowl, or outside if it was a nice day like today, and start popping away. I'm surprisingly slow with my little fingers. I realise that I must have slowed her down every week with this, but she never said anything and always let me help. It suddenly makes me feel special. I get two green beans to slice up too. Only two because I have to be careful with the knife, my mam tells me. When everything is cooking, the whole house smells amazing.

It's only twelve o' clock and already I've fed horses, had a lovely walk with my dad, played hopscotch, and helped my mam prepare vegetables. All the worries I had about coming back this morning have gone away.

We sit and eat our dinner at the table before watching *The Waltons*, everyone's favourite family programme back then, followed by *The Little House on the Prairie*. Dad usually takes a nap on his favourite chair after food and Mam enjoys an afternoon film. There was usually an old musical to watch on a Sunday afternoon. We'd all be too full to do much else so I would watch it with her. Today it's *Chitty Chitty Bang Bang*. That child catcher used to give me the heebie jeebies, still does. I kick off my shoes, climb onto the sofa next to my mam, and immediately feel safe.

14

Mam says she'll take me to watch the jazz band competition next weekend and we can have a look around the stalls. That's where we got Amber from, my teddy bear. Someone was having a jumble sale and we got it there. I'm excited to see my old teddy again, I didn't think I would be that bothered.

I'll just take the old necklace today. I know my parents won't miss it because there was a broken chain on it. My dad planned on throwing it away. He had other items he wanted to keep instead so he was getting rid of some of the broken ones. I hope he doesn't regret it. There are quite a few things I got rid of from my past that I wish I had kept now.

I could do with a good nap after that dinner, but what eight-year-old sleeps in the day? My mother would probably think I'm getting sick and give me some disgusting medicine. I go and sit on the steps in the front yard, just to have a look around. I'm hoping that the fresh air will wake me up a bit. As I sit there with the smell from the traditional roast dinners still lingering in the air, I think about how many times I've sat here in the past. As a child with my friends, resting after a fall, as a teenager just wanting some alone time.

A memory of my friends and I playing *Spirit in the Glass*

edges into my thoughts. We used to play it out in the dark, here on these steps. I smile as I think about the times we would scare each other and end up running indoors. Someone would move the glass or the wind would blow the letters all away and we would scatter with them. I was allowed to stay out a bit later sometimes as long as it was just on the steps, no further than the gate.

There were less trees around the village at this time so you could see the mountains better. There are only three old cars parked in the street now and not a single car has passed by in the last ten minutes. In the present day, this is a main road full of cars parked up on both sides. You couldn't play a game of rounders on the street today like we used to. I take a walk around to the back of the house where the vegetables are that my dad had planted. Most gardens looked the same back in the seventies: vegetable patches, some flowers, and a clothesline usually above a path through the middle of the garden, with an old wooden stick to prop it up. I used to carry the pegs out and pass them to my mother when she was hanging our clothes out to dry.

Just behind my house was the comprehensive school that I went to. Now that's a site I don't miss at all. Somehow it looks smaller now, less intimidating.

I feel a bit more refreshed after being outside, like I've got my second wind as my mother would say. When I go back inside, Lisa and Mary are here.

Two encounters in one day. What did I do to deserve this? Had I known, I would have stayed outside for a while longer. I stand still wondering if anyone has seen me yet, but they have so I just sit down and pretend to seem interested while Lisa plays with my Sindy dolls and narrates to me as she's playing. She's probably expecting me to kick off because she's taken all the best dolls, but she doesn't know that I really couldn't give a toss today. This is going to annoy her even more, seeing that I'm not phased. She's getting louder now just to bug me. Listening to her screechy voice is like nails on a chalkboard.

All I want to do is stick my sweets in her hair like little decorations that she can't get out, but I keep smiling and offer her some more sweets. After she's eaten a few more she tells my mother that I'm not sharing with her so I end up having to give her even more. I guess I never gave her the credit she deserves, she's an evil genius.

I've been outsmarted by a kid and I feel like I'm being treated unfairly. I get up and ask if it'll be teatime soon.

"Almost," Mam replies.

"So can Lisa go home now?" I ask.

I'm eight, I'm allowed to be a little impolite. What I don't say is that I want her out of the house before I kick her out. Of course, I get told off for being rude to our neighbours but I'll get over it. I have to pretend to be a little upset though, so I pout for a bit.

"If the wind changes, your face will stay that way mind," Mam says and we both smile. I miss the old sayings. A lot of them didn't really make sense but they were funny. I never believed that eating bread crusts would make your hair curly either and I didn't want curly hair anyway, so that one backfired on them. I can't believe how much Lisa got to me earlier. I wish I hadn't let her push me around so much in the past. I'm glad they moved away before we became teenagers.

Teatime is a treat of treacle pudding and custard, followed by little jam tarts topped with sponge. My stomach and heart feel full today and I still have my potato and sprout sandwich to look forward to later. I play a game of cards with my dad on the sofa while the top forty plays on the old radio. One or two of my old favourites were in the charts that day. *Forever Autumn* by Justin Hayward, which I still love today, and *You're The One That I Want* from the film *Grease*, which I've seen about a hundred times now. Number one was *Three Times a Lady* by the Commodores, which I found boring and too slow as a child. Mam is putting away the pile of dishes she has just washed and dried, making me wish I'd helped out more when I was younger. I think she appreciates that my dad keeps me occupied while she does that so that I'm not harassing her while she's busy. The music seems to keep her spirits up while she's doing it, she sings along happily.

When she serves up our supper I feel as tired as my mam looks, it's been quite a day. My potato and sprout sandwich is amazing. It feels like new taste buds are awakening especially for it so that I can fully appreciate the flavour.

I don't know how much longer I can stay awake, so I give my mam and dad a hug and tell them I'm tired and ready for bed. I think I could sleep standing up right now. I go into their bedroom and into the old dressing table drawer to get the necklace. I pause to have a quick look at all the old jewellery before I leave. The old lockets were stunning. I have some of these now in my jewellery box back at home, left to me by my dad. I don't wear them often; I worry about losing them.

I've had the most amazing day here today, despite Lisa, but now it's time to leave.

15

I get back to the present, go downstairs, and collapse onto the sofa where John is sitting with Chewy. Chewy runs up onto my chest and licks my face like he hasn't seen me for a year. He does this anytime we get back from anywhere. I'm so glad he's just a little dog.

John asks if today went okay when my Chewy attack is over. I rest my head on his shoulder and tell him I have the necklace now too.

"Did you get something nice for dinner for yourself?" I ask.

"Yes, I treated myself to a Domino's pizza. I'm still stuffed. Did you get your lovely roast dinner and sprout sandwich?"

"Course I did. I forgot to watch how the Yorkshire pudding was made though."

"Don't worry, you can just keep trying, it's fun to watch. And it might actually turn out right one day by accident." We both can't help but laugh. We know there's a very slim chance of that happening.

I'll meet up with Sara and Daniel tomorrow and ask if John can go back next. They should be pleased that I've already got two of the items.

I tell John about how much Lisa got to me today. He reminded me that when I talked about my past before I rarely mentioned Lisa so I couldn't have spent much time with her, and I realise he's right. I had other friends in the street that I spent more time with, nicer ones. Today was just unlucky regarding her, everything else was perfect.

Chewy has gone to settle down in his bed which means it's almost bedtime for us. If we don't move by eleven o'clock then he'll just get back up and sit in front of me and stare, like he's trying to say, 'You do know it's bedtime, right?' It's funny watching this one-foot-tall creature trying to intimidate me, but he looks so serious sometimes that I have to give him the win. We all need one now and again and he looks so pleased with himself when he gets it.

John pulls me up from the sofa as I don't have the strength to get up myself. I'm too tired and I really don't want to move.

I try to get ready for bed as quickly as possible. I can't wait to feel the softness of the quilt draped over me. I forgot about the exhaustion when I get back. I'm glad I didn't join in with the game of rounders in the street today, I think I would be glued to my bed all week.

John picks a film quickly tonight, we're both tired and hope to just go straight to sleep. He snuggles into me while we both drift off. I couldn't feel more comfortable if I were wrapped in a cloud. I go to sleep with a tired smile.

16

Sara

"I've just had a text from Marie. She wants to meet up today with an update. I said we'll meet her in the café at ten."

"That sounds promising then," Daniel says. "Maybe she's got another item. You know if she gives us the teddy today that we still have to see it through to the end though, right? We still have to honour the contract she signed to go back for three items and let John go back one day."

"I know. Although it would be tempting to just pull out and disappear, she'd never find us anyway. She probably wouldn't even try."

"We can't do that to them," he replies.

Daniel gives me a look that I've seen a lot of lately, like I'm being quietly judged for being too harsh or unfeeling. He never used to look at me like that before we took this job.

"We won't," I assure him, "but I will feel better when she hands the vial over to us."

"The vial doesn't contain the virus, it's just a part of the mixture. It's not dangerous on its own," he says.

"I know, I'm not worried about anything happen to them," I reply. "I'm just worried about something going wrong and us not getting it."

There it is, that look again. I hate when he looks disappointed in me like that. I need to remember to keep calm and keep my feelings in check until this is all over.

"That sounded a bit harsh," he says.

"Did it? I didn't mean it to."

Despite what Daniel may think, I'm actually looking forward to meeting up with Marie today. She's been a lot easier to get along with since our first encounter. It'll take my mind off things a little. As much as I like her though, I don't think I would want her life. She's got no money for a start. That may sound a bit unkind, but I just don't want to live like that. It's fine for her if she doesn't need it to be happy, but I'm not like that. I know Daniel could be.

Even when Marie does get the money, I doubt she'll make the most of it. I can't see her going on expensive shopping sprees or anything like that, I think she'll still be a bargain shopper.

I just can't imagine living like that when you don't have to. I want to buy designer outfits and live luxuriously. I want to enjoy my life, and I want people to notice me when I walk past them.

Maybe I should ask Marie to come shopping with me one day, get her all dressed up and have some fun. I think she would look quite different in a nice dress and a bit of makeup. A girls day out shopping sounds like fun too and I don't really have anyone else to do that with. I could probably tolerate a bargain buy or two. I would draw the line at second hand though. The thought of wearing something that's touched someone else's skin doesn't sit well with me.

Daniel thinks he knows me so well but if he knew more of my pet peeves, I think he would run for the hills and never look back.

17

Marie

I lay in bed for a while this morning thinking about yesterday. It was nice seeing my parents again at that age. I have a greater appreciation now for everything they did for me. They made life seem so simple back then, even though they worked so hard.

My mother took so much pride in the housework. Most of the men had worked in the mines, especially when they were younger. That's why these villages were built, for the miners. I wonder how they found any time to just enjoy themselves.

It felt good whenever I helped my mother bake or get a fire ready to be lit, or when I helped my dad plant seeds and pick vegetables. I wanted to be like them.

John brings a cup of tea and some biscuits up to bed for me.

"I remember how tired you were when you came back last time, but don't get used to it," he says with a smile.

I shuffle up the bed to have my tea and John sits down next to me.

"I had such a good day yesterday. I hope you enjoy yours too. I'm gonna try to get you back next time. Have you thought about when you want to go back to?"

He pauses for a moment to think.

"Remember you can't bring anything back," I say, "so you don't need to pick whenever you had your beloved Dr Marten boots. Buy a pair instead, cheapskate. Treat yourself when we get paid."

The disappointing look proves I was right, that is what he was thinking about.

"Okay, so I might go back to when I was about eight."

"Any special reason?" I ask.

"It was when I got my first bike," he replies. "I always wanted a Chopper bike but my dad couldn't afford a second hand one so he bought me a Pepper bike. It was a cheaper but very similar looking version. I was a bit disappointed at first that it wasn't a Chopper, but it was gold and looked the same, so I didn't mind."

"That sounds like a good day to go back to then," I say. "We'll check with Sara and Daniel this morning and hopefully you'll be able to go tomorrow if you want to."

"Okay, you'd better get up soon and get ready then. It's almost nine o'clock now," John says.

"I suppose I should move. I'll take a quick shower now and get ready."

"Don't lay back down then or you know you'll nod back off to sleep," John says before going back downstairs. It is tempting but he's right, I would be straight back to sleep today.

I look at the tea caddy and necklace that I'll be handing over this morning and realise I haven't even thought of the one thing I can bring back for myself yet. There's so much to choose from. I'll have to think about that soon. This decision would be so much easier for John, he'd pick his boots in a heartbeat.

18

Daniel

"Are you ready to go and meet Marie and John?"

"Yes, I just need to grab my purse and we can go," Sara replies. "I'll get some breakfast there."

She seems like she's in a better mood this morning, I hope today goes well. She's wearing the perfume I bought her for our three month anniversary, which she hasn't worn in a long time.

We get to the cafe fifteen minutes early. Sara orders a cheese and ham toastie and a coffee. I had breakfast before she got up this morning so I just order a coffee.

Marie and John arrive just as Sara is finishing her sandwich. Marie introduces us to John and they sit down after ordering their tea.

"So, what's the latest?" Sara asks, a little too eagerly. "How are things progressing?"

"Really good so far," Marie replies. "I've got the tea caddy and the necklace, I've brought them with me today. I've only got the teddy bear to collect now. I haven't come across that yet, but I probably will soon."

Sara quickly hides the disappointment from her face when

Marie says she doesn't have the teddy yet.

"That's great, Marie," I tell her. I'm impressed by how smoothly this is going so far. It feels like the finish line is in sight now.

"I want John to go back tomorrow. You said he could go back by himself one time and I've already brought back two of the three items, so I'd like him to have his turn before I go back for the last one," Marie says.

Before Sara gets a chance to mull it over, I tell Marie that it's fine, John can go back next.

"Thanks for letting me do this," John says.

I can see it means a lot to him. Marie tells us a bit about her visits and she smiles the whole time. I'm glad she's enjoying it. It makes me feel a bit better since we're not being entirely honest with her. They seem like a nice couple, they're probably better off not knowing. That's one thing Sara might be right about, but I wish she wouldn't talk like there could be trouble if they knew. It makes it sound like there's something shady going on, even though she insists there isn't.

It leaves me wondering if we're in danger, or if Marie and John are in danger.

John and I end up chatting about old cars from the past, while Marie and Sara talk about the fashion. It's been a while since I've seen her this relaxed and enjoying someone else's company.

I like Marie and John, they seem really nice and easy to get along with. They're in no danger of ending up like Tina. She shouldn't have threatened Sara.

Over an hour has passed when Marie says they have to go. She gets up, grabs her jacket off the back of the chair, and hands over a bag to Sara. Sara takes a look inside, checks the contents, and thanks Marie for them.

"We'll be in touch soon," Marie says before her and John leave.

When we get home Sara seems quite happy with their progress. I thought she would be angry that she hasn't got Amber yet, but I think she trusts Marie more now. Not that she's ever had a reason not to. She rings Liam with an update and the call is short and sweet so I'm guessing he's content for now too. Sara spreads out comfortably on the sofa like she's at ease for the first time in a while.

"Do you think we're doing the right thing letting John go back next?" she asks.

"Yes, I do. Marie seemed tired today, it'll be good for her to take a couple of days off before going again. It sounds like she had a great time revisiting her past."

"When would you go back to if you had the chance?" Sara asks me.

"Back to when I met you in college. I would have taken you on a date sooner, instead of wasting all that time apart." I squeeze in beside her on the sofa and she shifts a little to give me some room.

She seems lost for words but then says, "I would too. I don't know what's been wrong with me lately. I've just been thinking about how different we are sometimes, and it scares me that you'll realise it too and leave. I could get up one morning to an empty bed and home and never see you again."

"That will never happen. Not all couples have to have the same interests. I know you sometimes worry that I think you're shallow, but I don't. It doesn't bother me that you want nice things, there's nothing wrong with that. I want you to have them. Is there anything else you're not telling me? Work seems to get you really stressed at times."

"No, there's nothing else. I just want to get paid and not have to work again, and we're so close to that now," she says.

"I know." I still feel like she's not being entirely honest with me, but talking like this, it feels like the old us again.

19

John

Today is my turn to go back. I'm nervous and excited. My hands are so jittery that I almost spill my tea. I sit with Marie on the sofa and ask what her plans are for the day.

"I'm just going to do some tidying upstairs this morning and maybe read a bit later. My wardrobe needs a sort out too. I might treat myself to a few new things when we get paid."

"You might as well spoil yourself a little. Everyone deserves to treat themselves once in a while. Maybe you could ask Sara to go with you," I suggest.

"I think her taste is a little too expensive for me," she replies. "I don't want to spend silly amounts of money on clothes. Maybe I could show her how satisfying getting a bargain can be. What do you think?"

"I can't see that happening," I say.

I try to hide how nervous I am, but I think Marie sees it. She touches my hand and says, "You'll be okay. Remember what you told me, just enjoy it."

"I will. I'm going to leave now before I change my mind. Enjoy your day, I'll see you later."

And after mocking Marie for going to the bedroom to

leave, I do exactly the same thing.

I arrive in my bedroom in 1972, in the two-bedroom flat that we lived in. It doesn't exist anymore; they were all knocked down a few years back. The bedroom is surprisingly big for a flat and I have quite a collection of cars and Lego in here. My two-year-old sister, Sharon, slept in my parents' bedroom next door.

She's already awake and making enough noise to wake the block. There are six flats here, and her voice can probably reach all of them. As my mother would say, "she had a bell in every tooth".

I go into the living room where I can smell porridge cooking. My dad and sister are both already up, sitting in the living room. My parents look so different, it's quite a shock seeing them like this again. It's like watching an old photograph suddenly come to life. A big smiles appears on my dad's face when he sees me, I can tell he's been eagerly waiting for me to get up so he can give me my new bike.

"I've got a surprise for you today. I wanted to give it to you before I go to work." I forget it's just a normal day to them. He worked in the coal mine in Abergwynfi as a winder, taking the men up and down to the mines.

My dad brings in my Pepper bike and I can tell he's been looking forward to giving it to me all morning. I try to look surprised.

"It's great dad, thanks. I'll take it out after breakfast. Can we leave it in the passage for now?" That way Sharon won't be able to get her grubby little hands on it and cover it with dribble.

Mam dishes us up a lovely bowl of porridge each, adding a drizzle of creamy cold milk on the top to cool it down a little. Then she sits down to feed Sharon, who has already got it all over her hands after trying to grab the spoon. I made the right decision about keeping the bike away from her.

I'm not really in a rush to get out. I want to just sit here for a while with my parents. I feel like I'm sitting on the set of a classic TV show with everything around me being so old.

The flats here were quite spacious apart from the kitchen, but it was big enough. It had one of those olds pantries where you could fit just about everything in. They were like a Tardis. There were three blocks of flats here and just in front was a narrow river that travelled all the way down the valleys to the town of Port Talbot. There was a pipe we used to climb across to get over to the other side of the river to play. Not that there was much over the other side, it was just fun to try and get across without falling in and getting wet.

It was a lovely neighbourhood to live in, there were lots of other children living here so I always had friends to go out with. The adults always took care of the appearance of the blocks, taking turns to clean the steps and hallways on the weekends.

My dad asks if I want to go outside now to try the bike for a bit before he goes to work. My mother insists I put my coat on because it's not very warm today. I think she's a little surprised when I don't argue about it. I forgot that eight-year-olds usually acted like it was the end of the world having to wear a coat, especially on a bike, and I didn't even protest. It's confusing trying to remember that you're supposed to act like a child. I take it off and put it on the wall outside as soon as I get out the front. My dad says he won't tell as long as I put it on if I get cold.

I ride my new Pepper around the front lane while my dad watches with a huge smile on his face. He looks as happy as I am. Alan from the next block comes over to have a look and asks for a turn. He has his own bike and lets me ride it sometimes so I can't say no.

My dad goes back in to get ready for work while I stay out with Alan. We're not on a proper road, just a lane leading up to the flats so we don't have to worry so much about traffic. Not that we worried about things like that anyway, we were just thinking about how fast we could go. I can go pretty fast on this Pepper bike.

My dad is leaving for work so I give him a big hug when he comes out. I don't want to let go. He probably thinks it's because I'm so grateful for my present today. I would go to work with him if I could.

My mother is soon calling me to come in for a sandwich and some crisps for dinner. Luckily I had already remembered to put my coat back on before she came out.

I tell my mam that I'll be going back out on my bike after I finish watching Scooby Doo so she asks me to watch Sharon while she puts a few clothes away in the bedroom. I say okay while I watch Sharon play with the coal bucket. She looks so funny now, trying to walk around with it on her head.

I don't want to be kept in so I shout in to my mam, "Sharon has got the coal bucket, she grabbed it too quick for me to stop her."

My mam comes rushing in to find Sharon's blonde hair now covered with what looks like a dusting of black snow, and her face is like a gothic clown. I do feel a bit guilty now though that my mam has to bath her straight away, which means another chore for her to do today. I ask if she wants me to get anything from the shops for her while I'm out. I guess when we were that young we never considered the consequences of some of our actions for our parents.

She writes me a small list and gives me money for sweets too, which I feel slightly guilty for taking. I probably don't deserve it after making more work for her. I climb the steep path around the back of the flats that lead up to the main street of the village, which back then was filled with different shops and businesses. There were clothes shops, shoe shops, and even a bank. I go to the Co-op, they'll have everything she needs on her list. It takes me almost ten minutes to pick sweets because there's so many I haven't had in years. I settle on a bag of Gold Rush, a yellow stringed bag filled with little yellow nuggets of bubble gum, and a quarter of cola cubes. Then I get my mother's shopping before heading back home.

The scenery is so different today, I can see all around the village. There are less trees blocking the views compared to how it is now.

After dropping off my mam's shopping, I take my bike out again and give Alan a shout so we can race down the lane. I actually feel like an eight-year-old again speeding down the lane on my new bike. I could do this all day, until it's time to leave. We spend all afternoon competing for the fastest time. It goes so quickly though. I can already hear my mother calling me in again for teatime. I was having so much fun, apart from the one time I did come off and graze my hands, but that was relatively mild to some of the other crashes I had when I was a kid.

My mam takes a look when I get in and gently washes out any dirt that may have gotten in the skin, which stings a little. She dries them before serving me beans on toast, my favourite.

Sharon has fallen asleep mid-mouthful of beans. It's the only time she's quiet, when she's eating or sleeping. Mam has to wake her to finish what she's eating though, so it doesn't last. It's nice and cosy in front of the fire. I'd forgotten how cold the bedrooms were back then with no central heating.

The time has gone so fast today, it's gone by in blur, but it has been nice to revisit my past. Like Marie said though, it doesn't feel like you belong anymore because things have changed so much, even though some things are better back here. There was so much community spirit.

Sharon's eyes closing in between mouthfuls is getting hypnotic to watch, I didn't even realise how tired I am. My mam will stay up late tonight. She waits for my dad to come home from his afternoon shift to cook him some supper. We settle down on the sofa once Sharon is asleep to watch *It's a Knockout*. We have some biscuits while Mam has a cup of tea before I get sent to bed. I wonder what Marie is doing right at this moment. I picture her reading on the sofa with Chewy cwtched up at the side of her. She'll be in her pyjamas, her hair still damp and wavy from the shower. She'll probably be wondering if I'll be returning soon. I suddenly have the desire to get back there right now. I get what she means about feeling a million miles apart.

As I say goodnight and head off to the bedroom after giving my mam a hug, I realise I can't say any of the things I really want to say, because eight-year-olds don't talk like that. So I just take one last look and know that I'll remember her better like that now, now that it's fresher in my mind. So I did get a gift to take back after all. I get a better memory of my mam and dad when they were young. I won't forget my first day on my new bike again and I'm pretty sure I won't forget Sharon walking around with a coal bucket on her head for a while yet. I can already feel Marie's eyes rolling about that one.

When I get back, Marie is ready to put the kettle on and dish up some cake so we can sit down together and she can hear about my day. I can tell how relieved she is that I got back okay, and so am I. Back where I belong, with Marie.

20

Marie

John is still asleep when I get up. It took a while to wake him last night after he fell asleep on the sofa. I try to be as quiet as possible so I don't wake him yet.

I get a text from Sara asking if yesterday went okay and wanting to know when I'll be going back next. Considering they said there was no time limit at the start of all this, Sara can be a little overbearing. I tell her not today but maybe tomorrow, and that there's no guarantee tomorrow will be my last time. Hopefully that will keep her happy for a bit.

I want to at least go back to Christmas Day just once, and I want to go to that jazz band competition too. That's probably when I'll go next.

John appears just after ten and seems like he enjoyed a good sleep last night.

"I really enjoyed yesterday," he tells me. "You're right though, it did feel strange. But it was great to see my parents again and it's a long time since I've ridden a bike that fast. It was so much fun."

"I'll bet you were going faster than you probably should have been but I'm glad you enjoyed it. And what did you do to Sharon?" I just know there will be something.

"I'll tell you all about that later," he says with a grin.

"Shall we go for a drive somewhere today? You can tell me more about it then and we can stop off somewhere for food maybe."

"Yes, sounds good to me. We can nip down to the beach front and grab some chips from the fish shop. We can always eat them in the car if it gets too cold," he replies.

I prefer to eat them in the car anyway. We like to just sit in the car sometimes and enjoy looking around. We prefer to enjoy a nice view while we eat, rather than looking at the four walls of a cafe or restaurant.

John told me about the Sharon and coal bucket incident while we ate our lunch in the car at the seafront in Aberavon. I was not overly impressed, but it could've been worse and I couldn't help but laugh a little.

21

Sara

"So from what I got from Marie, John enjoyed his day back yesterday and she might be going back tomorrow," I tell Daniel.

He sits down besides me on the sofa.

"Okay, well don't get your hopes up yet. She might want a couple more times back before finishing this. I would, I mean there's so many days to choose from over the matter of a few years. She's bound to have a couple in her head," he replies.

"Yes, but I did say the other day it can't be dragged out too long. I think she'll do two or three more. Just the sooner she gets the next one done the closer to the end."

I can't let Daniel find out what Liam wants that vial for. I, for one, don't feel very safe lately knowing what I know. I just know that Liam had something to do with the accident last year with Tina. I think he knows I'm suspicious and that makes me feel even more vulnerable. I also don't like the way he looks at us sometimes, like we are dispensable. It's no wonder my head is all over the place. I feel so guilty about being a bit snappy towards Daniel lately too, but I just can't seem to stop worrying.

I don't even realise that I've been staring at Daniel while thinking about this.

"Why do I feel like you're evaluating me?" he asks.

"It's not you. I've been evaluating everything lately. I know I've been awful sometimes and you probably think I'm greedy talking about the money all the time. You know I'm not going to change though, right? It's not like I'm asking you to support me, but can you live with me like that and not end up resenting me for it?"

"I think I could, if you could cope with me being the casually dressed other half. I can deal with putting a suit on sometimes for special occasions or evenings at a restaurant but the rest of the time, I want to be in casual clothes and eat from a local chippy. Maybe even roam around the house in my pyjamas eating junk food, sometimes without brushing my hair," he says with a smile. "Can you live with me like that?" he asks.

"I think I could slum it for you," I smile back. "Plus, you look cute in your pyjamas. Let's just spend some quality time together once we've been paid. If we don't clash over the dishevelled hair and the designer clothing then I think there might just be hope for us yet. We could have that wedding we talked about before. But you do have to wear a suit for that," I say.

We snuggle up together and stay there on the sofa for a while.

***

Daniel

I like this opposites attract thing we have going at the moment. It makes our relationship feel even more special, like we can overcome anything to be together. I want Sara to have nice things. I want to shower her with gifts, and I will when we get paid. I love that she can accept me for who I am too. She doesn't need to know about my past. I'll be the loyal loving husband that she deserves. This is my chance to finally put everything behind me and look forward to our future together

Maybe I'll introduce her to my dad one day, I want him to be a part of our lives. It might help him recover and stay sober, especially if he had grandchildren to look forward to. He's always been a great dad, despite his problems, so I know he would make the best grandfather to our kids.

22

Marie

"Okay, I'm off to get Amber today," I tell John. "Or at least be there the day I get it. Not sure if losing it on the first day is a good idea. I want to leave early so I'll see you later, I shouldn't be too late back today." I leave John in the kitchen making toast. Chewy sits behind him with an optimistic look that means he thinks he's having toast for breakfast too.

It's only eight o clock so I won't have to rush to get ready. If I remember correctly, these things used to start around midday. The jazz bands would march through the main streets first on their way up to the football field at the top of the village, where they would parade around and play the bazookas and drums. At the front would be about three people twirling batons. Each team would have different colour uniforms, usually skirts or trousers with matching jackets and hats. They were judged on best performance with points lost for dropping a baton or missing a drum beat and not marching in sync. I used to love watching them every summer. Plus there will be jumble sale stalls there, which were always fun to look through.

When I get downstairs, Mam is putting the hoover around.

I remember the faded red apron that she is wearing this morning. It was her favourite one so she wore it a lot. She always had an apron on when she was indoors. The only time she didn't wear one was when she went out somewhere. All the women in the neighbourhood were the same. I guess it makes sense, as they spent most of their day busy with one thing or another.

Headscarves were quite popular too. They would fold them into a triangle, place it on their head, then tie it under their chin. My mother used to show me how to put one on. I remember she had some really lovely, patterned ones that I used to love putting on when I was playing dress up. I still remember her favourite was a blue patterned one with tiny tassels right around the edges. I wasn't allowed to play with that one.

She asks me to bring the milk in from outside for breakfast as she forgot to get it this morning. I hope the birds haven't got to it. Sometimes they would open the shiny foil tops if the bottles were left outside too long. The milkman was always around before we got up so it was impossible to avoid that happening now and again. That milk would then have to be poured away so that the bottles could still be washed, ready to put out in the evening for the milkman to collect again in the morning.

Luckily, this morning it's all okay. The weather looks great, the sun is already blazing down onto the silent street that'll be bustling later with jazz bands and spectators. I'll have to remember to wear sun cream later. If I burn I don't know if that would come back with me. I don't want to look like someone who's had a mishap at a tanning salon or overdone it with a bottle of fake tan.

It'll be just me and Mam going today, the men were never fans of these occasions. They all enjoyed the afternoon in their back gardens talking about seeds and vegetables, or watching a Western film on TV in peace. I'll have to get ready after my cereal, which I suppose means putting on a pretty dress again. I'm definitely picking a winter's day next time. I stay in my room for a bit when I go to get ready to look through some of my old things. I'm trying to decide what to take back with me for myself but, so far, nothing is standing out. I'd like to take everything.

"It'll be time to leave soon, are you nearly ready?" my mam calls up to me.

"Yes, Mam, I'll be down in a minute now," I reply.

I spot my old jewellery box, with the ballerina that spins around to music when you open the lid. It's white with red and pink roses around the edges. It's a little battered on the outside but the bright red velvet lining inside is still like new. It would look lovely on one of my shelves. I don't mind that it's a little worn looking, that's sometimes the appeal of vintage. I decide that this is what I want to take back with me. I know it's something I'll cherish.

"You look so pretty in that dress, Marie-Claire," my mam says when I go downstairs. She was the only one that called me that. One of my mam's favourite songs was *Where Do You Go to, My Lovely?*, so that's where my name came from. I like that she called me that sometimes. I'm not liking this dress very much though. Everyone dresses up to go to these competitions so I have the most nauseating pink frilly dress on. I can barely look at myself in the mirror without being conflicted between laughing at myself or crying. The latter came close, and now I can't unsee that image.

It's only a short walk to the field, but we sit outside and watch the jazz band teams marching through our street first. Then we, along with a crowd of neighbours from the street, follow behind them. Mam has a tub of fairy cakes to take with us. Everyone makes something and it all goes on to a table for everyone to eat later on after the competition.

Lisa is in one of the jazz bands so at least she's not annoying me today, not yet anyway. I could do without the grief today. My self-esteem is low enough right now in this pink monstrosity.

I end up joining a couple of old friends on the way there. We hold hands and swing them as we walk. It makes me feel like such a big kid but I need this, it reminds me I'm not the only one in a ridiculous outfit and the others don't seem to care so why should I. It's just for one day after all.

The field is already full of people getting things ready. It'll take a while to start so Mam takes me over to the jumble sales. That's where she spots my teddy bear. It's hard to miss as the bright orange stands out from anything else there, and it still looks new. She buys it without a second thought, before anyone else gets it. That's how it was at jumble sales, you had to be quick to get the best items. She knew I would like the bright colour of it.

I was so pleased and promised to take good care of it. She puts it in a bag to keep with her until we get home so that I don't lose it. She also gets a few handkerchiefs for my dad and some ornaments for her glass cabinet. The mams all chat away happily. It's nice to see them all enjoying themselves.

23

The competition starts and all the kids sit on the floor around the field, watching the performances in silence with the mams watching behind us. It takes about an hour to get through them all. There was always a good turn out of teams. Apart from a few mistakes from a couple of teams, they all do quite well. The top three are chosen and given their trophies before everyone goes over to the tables to get some food. There's so much choice. Mostly homemade cakes, sausage rolls, sandwiches, pasties, trifles, and lots of cocktail sausages with cheese and pickles. They knew how to put a spread on back then without it costing the earth. I'm quite hungry now so I fill my plate.

The air is starting to get chilly so we put our coats on, which I'm glad now that my mother brought with her. She looks like a movie star today, with her long dark hair pinned back at the sides, wearing her red dress and just a little bit of lipstick and foundation. I didn't get to see her like this often. It's like watching one of those lovely porcelain dolls that stood in a display case come to life.

I'm so glad when we get home that the fire is lit. I stand in front of it to warm my hands up. I didn't realise how cold I was until now. Mam runs me a warm bath while I sit down and tell dad about the competition and buffet afterwards. I know he's not really interested in those things but he nods along and smiles to show interest, just to make me happy. We brought some food home with us, as did everyone. There was so much left over. Mam says we can have it after my bath. I go upstairs and pick out some warm pyjamas while mam gives my teddy a check over to make sure it's clean enough for me to play with. I just know she'll be giving it a wipe over anyway, even if it does look clean.

My toes tingle when they meet with the warm water because they're so cold. Mam says she'll wash my hair tomorrow so I can leave it for today, which is fine by me. I feel so much better when I have my pyjamas on.

I sit down on the sofa with Mam and Dad and some of the food that we brought back home with us. I tell them I'm going to call the bear Amber because of the colour. I put it on the chair beside me, ready to take up to my bedroom later to keep on the bed. As I thought, it feels a bit damp on parts, like it's been washed down with a cloth. My mother always liked everything clean, especially if she didn't know where it came from. I can't really say I wasn't the same, so I just smile and pretend I haven't noticed.

This is lovely, just sitting watching TV with my parents, eating leftover party food in front of a glowing fire. I won't be taking Amber tonight, it's been such a lovely day. I can't say I lost my present the first day I got it, and how could I lose it without going anywhere. I'll be back another time for this one. I'm too cosy to move now so I'll probably be a bit later getting back tonight. Not too late though, I know John will worry.

24

John and I go out for a drive this morning to the top of one of the mountain roads just outside the village. We park in a lay-by and have some lunch that we brought with us. It's quite a view on a clear day like today, you can see for miles. It's nice to get some fresh air on the mountain before the weather gets too cold to do this.

I don't like spending too much time out of the car up here, there are too many big flies and wasps flying around. I usually end up looking like I'm learning some weird dance routine trying to dodge them all. Not great when there's a lot of traffic going by. John thinks I overreact with bugs and tells me I should try to chill out, but I'm really not capable of that. I've tried.

I once threw a bottle of pop at John because he asked me to pass it to him and I spotted a wasp on it. He was driving at the time so not my finest moment.

After our lunch, we just sit for a while and take a few photos of the view before heading back home.

I peel some potatoes when we get back ready to make a sausage dinner. John's still upset that he couldn't bring his old Dr Marten boots back from the past. He probably wouldn't find them comfortable to wear anymore anyway.

I did ask Sara and Daniel about the boots, but it was a no as I expected. It was always worth a try. I don't think my cooking will make him feel any better.

We call in to see my mam on the way home. It's so surreal seeing her young one day and old the next. I know she still misses my dad. I can't even imagine my life without John. We've been best friends for most of our adult life. He's always been the only one I can truly be myself with. We share mostly the same interests, and support each other with the ones that we don't share.

It's odd not being able to talk to my mam about travelling back in time. I probably will tell her one day, I don't know if she'll believe me though.

I remember we had a white Christmas in 1981, so that's what day I choose to go back to for my last visit.

25

Sara

I'll probably never get round to telling Daniel that it was no accident bumping into him that day after we hadn't seen each other in so long. I always liked Daniel and I knew he liked me too in college. I didn't want to do this by myself and I knew he would be the only other person I could count on to help me without asking too many questions. I'm not saying he's a fool or anything but he can be easily led, that's the impression I got of him in college. I had him wrapped around my finger in no time. Don't get me wrong, I do love him now and I do want us to have a future together. I just didn't know it that first day.

Things seem to be going well between me and him again. Marie and John are giving no cause for concern, and they are enjoying their times back in the past. Everything just seems to be going so well, I hope nothing spoils it now. I did even consider letting Marie bring those boots back for John but it had to be a no. I don't want them taking advantage and asking for more favours.

When I see Marie and John together, I find myself envying them a little. Their relationship just seems so much simpler than ours. I sometimes want to shake them to see if any glitter floats from them that I could sprinkle on me and Daniel. Maybe it would give us the magic that they seem to have.

Daniel says he's willing to accept my flaws, but we'll see.

When I think back to our college days, I think we didn't even realise how happy we were then, even though we were just friends at the time. I wish I'd been able to see into the future. I would have stayed clear of Liam and not involved Daniel in this whole thing. It's going to take a long time for me to make this up to him.

"Hey, you look deep in thought there. Is everything okay?" Daniel asks, as he comes into the living room.

"Everything's fine, thank you. I was actually thinking about how well things are going and what a lovely day it is today," I reply.

"That's good to hear. Things will be okay, you'll see. Pretty soon you'll be in your fancy dresses while I'm still in my jeans and t-shirt and we'll be the odd couple that match," he says jokingly.

While he goes to take a shower, I think about just handing everything over to Liam and walking out the door for the last time. I hope he won't expect anything else from us when this is all over. He won't get anything else. As soon that money is in my account, I'll be long gone, and me and Daniel can get our lives back.

26

Marie

"So, today will be a snow day for me," I tell John.

He reminds me how clumsy I am and tells me to be careful when I go outside.

I don't think I've ever met anyone as clumsy as I am. I've fallen down a few stairs and over a few walls, mostly when I was a kid and a couple of times after I'd had a few drinks. Maybe it should be illegal for clumsy people to drink alcohol, for health and safety reasons.

You see videos of people trying to walk in snow and just endlessly sliding and trying to stay upright while going down a hill, feet slipping all over the place the whole way down. That's like me going through life. Every step is a potential fall, every swallow of air a potential choking hazard. It's no wonder I'm a little superstitious, I need all the luck I can get. At least it's free entertainment for John and, as he says, there's no cost for his lifetime subscription.

"It will probably be my last day back today," I tell John, while really still trying to decide for sure.

We had a big blizzard on Christmas Eve in 1981. There was quite a few feet of snow on the ground by Christmas Day.

I have a compulsion to dress warmly which I know is silly as I'll have different clothes on when I get there, hopefully a nice warm pair of pyjamas. I shout down to John that I'm leaving.

I know he's going to enjoy spending most of the day with his online gaming today in peace. That's if Chewy doesn't nag him to play all day with his ball.

I feel the chill in the bedroom as soon as I get there. There were no double glazed windows in our house at that time and the bite of the frosty air would squeeze its way through the edges of the badly-fitted window frames. I want to stay snuggled under the quilt, but I want to see what it's like outside too. I find the courage to take the plunge to creep over to the bedroom window.

Wow, we really did get a lot of snow back then. My bedroom is at the back of the house and the snow drifts are sloping almost all the way up to my bedroom window. The back door must be completely blocked up. Can you imagine how strange that looks, opening the door to a wall of snow.

I love watching the snow sparkling in the sunlight, the different colours twinkling like diamonds on a white background. I don't know when the valleys looked more beautiful. It looks so different in every season, but equally as stunning in different ways. Now, as an adult, the wintry weather doesn't appeal to me as much. The village gets cut off from everywhere else and that can last for days.

I suddenly remember that it's Christmas Day. I was so distracted by the weather that I completely forgot that I have to get up and open presents. The first thing that catches my eye is the glowing fire that lights up the room. I can feel the warmth of it caressing my skin as I make my way down the stairs.

Mam and Dad are already both eagerly waiting for me to open my presents. They look more excited than me that I've finally emerged from my bedroom. I forgot how excited I used to get to watch our kids on Christmas Day. Of course it would be the same for them. The Christmas trimmings look so pretty; all bright, shiny colours spread across the ceiling, green, red and gold; tinsel spread around the room, twinkling like multi-coloured stars with the light reflecting from the fire; and cards hung on a piece of string like a garland across the wall. It's quite breathtaking.

It's not quite as big of a deal getting up early when you're eleven. You don't want toys anymore so it's all clothes and girly bits and pieces. I get some records and tapes, including the new *Top of the Pops* album which has Duran Duran and Siouxsie and the Banshees on. I still love the music from back then. We put that on to listen to while mam prepares our Christmas dinner. Dad helps her out with the dinner every Christmas Day. I sit in the kitchen with them for a while, before asking if I can go out until it's almost ready. I can see that the other kids in the street are out building a snowman at the side of the street. I put my big warm coat on with my scarf and gloves, which probably won't stay dry for long, and head out. The snow is like powder beneath my feet, with a barely audible crunch to it when my shoes dig in deeper. It's like battling an assault course just getting to the pavement. The steps are a challenge because they're not even visible anymore. There's just an uneven slope trying to entice me back down, but I don't give up.

There are a few of us out now and we build a fairly decent-sized snowman, about five feet tall. There's certainly enough snow around for it. By now I can't feel my hands and face, but I stay out a while longer. We all get called in eventually to have our Christmas dinner, which I've been looking forward to all morning. I want to save room for Christmas pudding later though. *The Sound of Music* is on TV, as it was every year on Christmas Day.

My dad's already nodded off to sleep so I snuggle up next to Mam in front of the still glowing fire and watch the film.

I wonder if I fall asleep in my bed here would I stay here forever? That wounds me to even think about. I know I'd miss the life I have now, in the present. It feels like my heart is being torn in two, but I still don't regret coming back here.

I nip upstairs to find Amber and get it ready to go back later. It's the last thing to collect now. I find it lying under a bunch of other old soft toys that I probably end up getting rid of soon anyway. We find it so easy to get rid of our old things when we're young, never even considering that we might regret it one day.

When I get back downstairs, a bowl of Christmas pudding with custard is waiting for me, mine and my dad's favourite. I eat it as slowly as I can to make it last longer. I like how the taste of food can sometimes remind you of certain places. If I ate this anywhere else and closed my eyes, I would feel like I'm right back here again.

I enjoyed being out in the snow today, the cold is more bearable when you're younger. You don't really notice it when you're enjoying yourself with your friends.

Me and Dad do a jigsaw puzzle together, one that I got as a present today with a picture of some cute puppies. Mam's watching the Christmas episode of *Coronation Street*. I get to stay up later on Christmas and I'm not in a rush to leave. Plus, there are tins of Quality Streets and Roses to get stuck into.

Dad bought mam her favourite perfume for Christmas and a new red floral headscarf. She bought him a nice woollen jumper and a couple of western books. When we sit down to a supper of turkey sandwiches, my mam says, "I'm surprised you didn't spend half the day upstairs playing music like you usually do after having new records."

"I didn't want to today," I tell her. "I can do that anytime."

She seems pleased to hear that, I see her smile to herself. It's nice to see that they also enjoyed today. I can go back happy tonight, knowing that they've had a lovely day too.

I know I can't stay, so I have to leave now, with this lovely last memory to take with me. Today was just perfect. I give them both the quickest hug and thank them for all my presents, then make a quick exit up the stairs to hide the tears filling my eyes like a dam that's about to burst.

I stand behind the bedroom door for a minute to settle myself. I don't feel guilty about taking money for this anymore. It feels like compensation for breaking my heart a little. I sit on the bed and listen to my dad's voice talking to my mother downstairs. I remember how tiring Christmas Day was as a parent. It's that contented kind of tired that you get after a good day, when the excitement is all over but you're still tingling from the little sparks of flashbacks. I want my dad's voice to be one of my last memories. I hear him say, "It's been a good Christmas, hasn't it? Marie-Claire seemed to enjoy," and I know it's time to leave. My dad never said my full name often, so it's a special last memory to take away. These last few days here have been unforgettable.

27

I don't go straight home today. I decide to take a detour first, to get John's boots. I don't think Sara and Daniel are being honest about not taking stuff back so I'm just going to do it anyway. What are they going to do, sack us? The job is finished anyway.

I know that John's mother used to leave a key inside their letterbox back in the past, a lot of people did that. I know a certain date that they were all out visiting relatives for John's auntie's birthday. I saw the photos and he wasn't wearing his boots that day. The house will be empty and I'll be able to slip in and take them. He'll just end up having a new pair so no big deal. That day was in 1986 so he would have already had the boots for two years. They actually lasted him through half of our marriage, until the soles finally gave out. He used to spend hours polishing them. If he paid the same attention to polishing his pool trophies, I wouldn't have minded him having so many.

I'm not really sure if going back to John's past will work, but I do what I usually do and put the date, time, and place into the wristband, and close my eyes. When I open them, I'm right outside John's old house wondering why I didn't put the location as inside the house. *What an idiot*, I think to myself. At least it's dark so there's less chance of being seen.

I look down and get distracted by my clothes. I'm wearing my favourite old jeans that I had when I was sixteen. They didn't last as long as John's boots unfortunately. I also have my burgundy leather jacket on. I try to look at my hair to see what colour it was that day. I know at one point I dyed my hair the same colour burgundy as this jacket. It'll either be that colour, or it'll be blonde. I used to dye it often back then but blonde was my usual choice until my twenties. It's burgundy now, as I suspected.

I suddenly feel a bit nervous at the thought of sixteen-year-old me sneaking into John's parents house. They wouldn't even know me yet. I can feel my heart rate picking up pace. I don't want to leave without the boots so I'll just do this as quickly as possible. Luckily, there's nobody around. I couldn't look any more shifty if I tried. I just slip my hand through the letterbox and grab the key. It's such a relief that it's where he said it would be because I'm dangerously close to hyperventilating right now. I open the door and close it quickly behind me. I try the count to ten thing to try to regain some kind of composure. It helps a little. A smile even tiptoes to the surface of my face when I think about how ridiculous I'm being right now.

I know exactly where the boots will be, upstairs in his bedroom by his bed. The stairs are just inside the hallway so I run up as fast as my shaking legs will take me.

The boots are right there, as I thought. I grab them and run back downstairs to look for a carrier bag. I want to hide them from John until tomorrow. I find a bag of carrier bags just inside the kitchen and take one out. As I'm leaving, something startles me. While my heart is racing like an F1 car, I realise it's the dog I forgot they had. It was just a little one but I bet those tiny teeth could do a bit of damage to my ankles if he felt threatened.

I quickly get out of the kitchen and shut the door behind me so that he can't get out.

I naively thought I would have a nose around and take a look at some old photos in the living room but sitting down calmly looking at photographs is really not on the cards. I'm desperate to leave and almost regret my decision to come here.

With my stomach still doing somersaults, I lock up and put the key back inside the letterbox. John had better be happy to see these boots. I've only just managed to keep down my Christmas supper from earlier, or from five years ago, I don't know anymore. I'm clearly not cut out for a life of crime. If a cop car pulled up right now I would be straight on my knees confessing to everything. Or, being me, I'd be more likely to end up panicking, throw the boots at them, hit one of the coppers and get done for assaulting a police officer with a Dr Marten boot. Things tend to escalate when you're clumsy like me and usually not in a good way. If John had lived at number thirteen, I wouldn't have even considered risking coming here at all.

I just need to compose myself, set my wristband, and get the hell out of here. I manage to steady my hands just long enough to get home.

When I get back, John is in the shower so I hide the boots under the bed for now. I know he'll be so happy to have them but it can wait until tomorrow. I have no energy left for anything else tonight.

As I'm drifting off to sleep, John kisses me goodnight. He doesn't ask about my day yet; he knows how hard the last visit would have been for me. He just says, "Goodnight, I'll see you in the morning," and we both quickly fall asleep.

28

I wake up and pick Amber up out of the bag beneath the bed, tuck it under my arm, and go back to sleep. I think about the lovely memories I have of yesterday while I drift back off to sleep.

John brings me a cup of tea an hour later.

"I'm glad you don't have to go back anymore. I mean, I know that you can if you want to until you hand the teddy bear over, but knowing you don't have to is a bit of a relief," he says.

"I won't be going back. You know how it felt to leave. Besides, I need you to show me how you look in these later," I say while pulling his Dr Marten boots out of the bag. To say he's pleased would be an understatement. His eyes light up like mine do when I see cake.

"How did you manage that?" he asks.

"Put your feet up on the bed, this could take a while," I tell him.

I tell him about my extra trip last night, which he finds hilarious. He said he would have loved to have been there to see how much of an idiot I must have looked sneaking around. I can't help but giggle a little. It'll be a while before I can really have a good laugh about it. I still feel a little shaken, and even though it makes no sense, I half expect the police to come knocking on the door. I just want to hide in the bedroom for the day like a fugitive. Maybe a shopping trip might help me take my mind off it.

"I would have kept them and wrapped them for Christmas if I'd known you were gonna be this happy to see them," I say. "If you feel like you can part with them for a bit later, maybe we could go shopping. Treat ourselves to something new? We'll be paid soon. Not for anything special, just maybe a new dress or something, I could get one for myself too," I joke. John rolls his eyes, like that's one of the worst jokes he's ever heard. It's not, all my jokes are lame. "We can see Sara and Daniel tomorrow, maybe. I'll give her a text later to see when they want to meet up."

"I wonder what Sara will ditch her yellow Fiat 500 for when she gets her big pay day," I say. "Something expensive and sporty I bet."

"A limo would be more her taste, I think," John replies.

"What about you, anything in particular you fancy going to have a look for today?"

"We'll just see when we get there."

I'm thinking John would like a bigger TV to go with his PlayStation, and I'd like more shelf space for my books. A reader can never have too many bookshelves. Maybe that's what we can look at today.

We get ready and leave to go shopping. John heads straight for the TV section just as I thought, and he's not surprised when I say bookshelves next. I know everyone says this, but I sometimes think we can read each other's minds. I have to stop somewhere to get some pastries and cakes, it wouldn't be a good shopping day without treats for later.

When we get back home and sit down, I remember thinking about those old pool trophies again. I ask John if he remembers the black and gold one that we both hated a little.

It was an awkward shape, heavy, and didn't match any of the other ones at all.

Neither of us will forget the night he had it. At the presentation, John must have thought that my eyes were filling up because I was so overwhelmed that he had won, but the tears that I was choking back was me thinking about the dust that trophy was going to gather. I could tell by the expressions of all the other wives that they were feeling the same way, and in solidarity, we all gave each other a sympathetic smile. John got so drunk by the end of the night it took him over half an hour to get upstairs from the living room. He kept trying to crawl up the stairs on his hands and knees and sliding back down on his stomach whenever he almost reached the top. That's what he got for squeezing in a few extra shots at the end of the night. Luckily, I didn't have quite as much to drink. He did surprisingly remember a lot from that night, all that throwing up was probably hard to forget. I don't think he ever drank that much again. John wants me to tell him my boots-stealing story again in bed so he can have a laugh before we close our eyes.

29

Sara

"I've got a meeting with Liam today," I tell Daniel as I drink my coffee.

"How come I'm never asked along to these meetings when we're both working on the same thing?" he asks.

"I don't know. Maybe he just thinks you wouldn't be interested in the small, boring details. We don't really discuss much, it's more of an update on how things are going, that's all. I can ask him if he could include you next time if you like, but you're really not missing anything."

"No, it's okay, I was just wondering. It doesn't sound like I need to be there. He must be getting excited about getting to work on this treatment or cure now that it's the last item to collect," Daniel says.

"I guess so. He doesn't really give a lot away, he just discusses details of our job to me," I say while rinsing my cup and wondering how Daniel can be so naïve. "I won't be there long anyway, so I'll see you when I get back."

I hate going to see Liam, I always have a nervous feeling in the pit of my stomach. I never used to feel like this at the beginning.

I sometimes even suspect that he's having me followed. I get that uneasy feeling that makes you constantly look over your shoulder. A presence that shouldn't be there.

"How are we on this last vial?" Liam asks. No hello, have a seat or anything.

"I think we'll have it sometime this week. As soon as we get the teddy bear."

"The quicker it's handed over the better so once you receive it just drive straight from pick up to here with it."

"Ok sounds good to me," I say.

I've always been curious, so I pluck up the courage to ask, "Where did you get the wristband and all this information anyway?"

"I heard about it on the grapevine. All this stuff really was from some kind of organisation. I found two of the guys that worked there, listened in to a few conversations and followed them around. Then me and some of my guys stole everything from them one day, the wristband and the list of names and items." He says this all so casually while looking through some papers on his desk.

"But how do you know that what they bring back is the right stuff you're looking for?"

"Because it said on all the paperwork we stole. Is there anything else you want to know? Why are you asking anyway?" He looks up at me, eyebrows furrowed slightly with frustration at my sudden curiosity. I regret asking now.

"No, I was just wondering that's all."

"Well, don't forget, curiosity killed the cat," he smirks, staring right through me.

And on that note, I leave.

When I get back home – I call it home but not for much longer as we'll be out of here as soon as we're paid – Daniel is cooking me a meal. There are candles and flowers laid out on the table.

"What a lovely surprise," I say. "What's cooking, it smells lovely?"

"Your favourite, fresh salmon, new potatoes, and baby peas, and I've got some black forest cake for dessert," he says.

"That sounds perfect, just what I need. I didn't realise how hungry I was until now."

"I can't promise this kind of service every day but I'll do my best if you're still considering me as your husband," he says with a big smile.

"I will have to give it some serious thought," I say, also smiling.

He just answers with a kiss.

"We can meet up with Marie and John tomorrow and have this done in the next day or two," I tell him.

I think once this is all done, the lies should be buried forever. Daniel will never have to know what I know. I could lose him if he did. He would never knowingly go along with being involved in selling something that could endanger lots of lives. I keep telling myself that it's not a certainty that that will happen, but I don't really believe it.

We enjoy a lovely evening meal and a few glasses of wine, while all these thoughts weigh heavily on me.

30

Marie

We're going to meet up with Sara and Daniel today to give them Amber, then we're all done. This last week has gone by so quickly, but what a week it's been.

"What time are we meeting Sara and Daniel?" asks John.

"I said about ten o' clock, is that okay?"

"Yes, that's fine," he replies. "I might take a look at a nice transporter van tomorrow for our little trips around the valleys. Something to think about when we get paid."

"I think that's a good idea," I say. "We may as well spend some of the money, and it should be on something that we'll probably get a lot of use out of."

We get to the cafe around the same time as Sara and Daniel, meeting them in the car park on the way in. They both look as happy as we are to be doing the last handover. The cafe now suddenly seems low-key for the occasion. Maybe we should have celebrated at a bar or something. I could've done with a strong cocktail last night.

I take Amber out for one last look, before I hand it over. If I could have, I would've chosen to keep this for myself. It has so many memories for me.

"So, what's next for you two?" I ask them.

Daniel tells me that they're going away for a week or two, then they'll return to discuss where they want to live more permanently. The smile never leaves his face. I really hope it works out for them.

"How about you two?" he asks.

"We'll be staying in the village, but we'll probably treat ourselves to a few new things with the money. I suppose that sounds dull and boring to you both."

"It doesn't sound boring to me at all," says Sara, who looks as surprised as us that she said that. "I mean, it must be nice to feel settled and know what you want. My parents were like that."

She gets out her laptop and transfers our payment to our bank account. I check to see if it's gone through okay. It has, to our relief.

"Shall we stay for food?" asks John. "I'm a bit hungry."

We all say yes and ask for a menu. Sophie looks glad of our custom, it's very quiet here this morning. I'll leave her a bigger tip today. I want to do something nice for someone else to celebrate.

"You'll have to give us a ring when you get back, let us know where you decide to move to," I say to Sara and Daniel.

"Yes, that would be great. We'll do that," Daniel replies

I bet we'll never hear from them again though. I feel unexpectedly relieved, like we've just had a narrow escape.

We don't stay for long after our meal. Sophie protested a little about the tip but I convinced her to take it.

Sara can't get away quick enough. I might be offended if it was anyone else, but it seems about right for Sara. Daniel is more reluctant to leave, but gets dragged away. So we leave it at, "We'll call you one day."

When me and John get home, I take a piece of old chalk out of the drawer and ask him if he wants to play a game of hopscotch. He looks at like he's thinking, *Is she serious?*

"Just think of it as exercise," I tell him. "Come on, it'll be fun. Just this once, before we forget what it was like to be that young again."

31

Liam

"Where the hell are they?" I yell at my two employees, Neil and Tony.

I've been pacing back and fore my office for two hours now, waiting, and waiting, and waiting, but nothing. No sign from either of them. No phone call, no messages. I know they went to get that teddy bear hours ago. They should be here by now. She better not have run off with it. She was asking a lot of questions yesterday and she knows what it's worth.

"I want you both looking for her car, it shouldn't be too hard to spot. It's a yellow Fiat 500. Do you think you can both manage that?" I yell, slamming my fist into my desk.

They look at each other like I've gone mad, before turning back to me, open-mouthed like the morons they are, and nod in unison.

"Well, go on then, what are you waiting for? Go and find them."

"Yes, boss."

They can't get out of here quick enough.

I don't believe this is happening. Sara is really pushing her luck. She can't seriously think she'll get away with this. I know I never told her any details about my buyers, maybe she's got her own lined up. I should've watched her more closely. Maybe she got rid of that Tina woman that she kept going on about, the one who was giving her a hard time. Wouldn't surprise me now.

I clear my desk with one swift swipe of my arm. My secretary can clean that up tomorrow. I sit heavily back down in my chair. I need to slow my heart rate back down. I take one of my pills and go over details of my meetings with Sara in my head, trying to think if I missed anything obvious. Nothing stands out. She always behaved like a scared little rabbit, flinching at my every threat. It doesn't make sense to me that she would do this. Nobody is that good of an actor, surely.

32

Marie

We decided to splash out on a takeaway this evening and pick a film to watch on TV. We go with fish and chips and settle down to watch *50 First Dates*. I don't have vinegar on my chips this time, I still can't shake off the memory of wearing it the other day. I swear I can still smell it all the time. It's like someone poured it inside my nose and it's there to stay.

As it's a special evening, John gets on board with my vinegar embargo and doesn't have any on his food either. It won't last though. I know next time he'll have them covered in it and will be wafting them under my nose while asking if I want to smell them. Chewy watches us with great expectations but chips make him sick and he doesn't like fish, so we can't share with him. His food dish is full, but he'll still sit there now with the saddest look on his face, like he's posing for a dog's charity poster. I give him ten out of ten for his effort in trying to make me feel guilty. Maybe I'll get chicken next time.

"Chewy knows how to make me feel guilty when I'm eating," I say to John. "Look at those sad eyes." We both say,

"Aww" together and laugh. Chewy sees this as a prompt to dive up onto us to soak up the attention he knows he'll get.

When the film finishes, we put the news on for a bit before going up to bed and the headline catches our attention. A car has gone through some railings on a quiet road just outside Swansea. The driver of the yellow fiat 500 is believed to have died at the scene. Me and John can't believe what we're hearing.

"It has to be Sara's car, right?" It's like time has just frozen while we try to process this. We were with her just hours ago listening to her and Daniel planning their future together. She was so young. We're both struggling to make any sense of it. They didn't mention if anyone else was in the car. Daniel can't have been there, he'll be devastated.

33

Liam

Here they come again, my two henchmen, idiot number one and two. My expressions probably don't hide my disdain for them. It's not that I just don't like them, I don't like anyone who works for me. The only person I trust is myself and my family, close family anyway. My wife has been sick and I want this money to take her to America for treatment. I've heard good things about it. She insists she doesn't need it, but I want to give her every opportunity for a good recovery if I can. Nobody here knows about this. They would think I'm soft and I'd lose all credibility with them. Plus, it's none of their damn business. I take another pill for my racing heart. All this worry is taking its toll. I blame Sara for this.

"Well?" I ask.

"Did you see the news? We tried to have a look but when we got near the car to search it, another vehicle stopped a few minutes after us," says idiot number two.

"Well, this is just great. I still can't believe that Sara would have the guts to cross me. The police will have that car now. The vial is gone for good."

"It could've been Daniel's idea," says idiot number two.

Now I know I've named him correctly.

"Daniel has less stones than a healthy gallbladder. Plus, he had no idea what it was. My buyers won't be happy, but they don't have to know yet. This is just between us. Were you seen sniffing around her car?" I ask.

Idiot number one shrugs. "I don't think so."

"Well, you'd better hope not. Can't say I'm sorry, that'll teach her to get in over her head. She must've been driving too fast trying to get away. You can have a look for Daniel tomorrow if I don't hear from him, see if he does know anything. You're no more use to me tonight so you can both get out and come back early tomorrow. And you'd better hope the police don't come knocking on my door or I'll be knocking on yours."

34

Daniel

After leaving our meeting with Marie and John, Sara and I drive on to another café closer to town. Sara says she wants to check things out before going to Liam.

She tears open the back of the teddy bear like her life depends on it as soon as she parks the car. She's frantically searching for the vial but there's no sign of it. I'm as shocked as she is, but I'm still taken aback by her sudden outburst.

"How the hell can that be?" she screams at me. "Did she bring the wrong one back? Where the hell is it? We're dead, both of us. You have no idea."

She's seriously starting to worry me now. I've never seen her like this, she's practically hysterical.

I try to put my arm around her to try to calm her down but she shoves me away.

"We have to go back and ask Marie what the hell is going on. I'm telling you, this isn't the right teddy bear, it can't be."

"You can't go and see them like this, you'll end up scaring them," I tell her.

"I couldn't give a shit right now, Daniel. I want that vial and I'll get it anyway I can."

"What the hell does that mean?" I ask.

My head is trying to make sense of what's going on.

"Are you saying you would actually hurt them? What the hell is this, Sara?" I yell at her.

"Liam wants to sell it to someone for a huge amount of money to create a virus. The buyers are not interested in a cure or saving lives. That's all I know, and he'll do anything to get it. Are you getting it now, Daniel? We're in big trouble here."

"And you knew about this the whole time without telling me?" I yell.

"Yes, I knew you wouldn't go along with it if you knew and I didn't want to do this by myself," she says still angry, but a little too casually.

She starts up the car and drives out of the car park. I tell her she can't go back to Marie's and John's. I try to get her to stop driving, but she won't listen to me. I reach over to grab the wheel, I have to do something. She's out of control, she just keeps going faster and faster.

The next thing I know, the car is no longer moving. We've veered off the road and gone through the barriers.

I carefully try to move. I don't think I'm seriously hurt. Sara has blood dripping down the side of her head and she groans as she slowly opens her eyes. It feels like everything is happening in slow motion.

35

"Shit," Sara says. "How are we going to get there now?"

I can't believe those are her first words after driving off the road. She doesn't even ask if I'm okay.

"We just crashed Sara, what's wrong with you? You need to go to hospital, your head is bleeding. You can't go to Marie's now."

"Who's going to stop me, Daniel? You?" she laughs.

I feel like I'm looking at a different person right now. Maybe this is who Sara was all along. She's just admitted to selfishly using me to keep her company in all of this, whatever this is. Between the crash and what she just said, my head is spinning too fast to make much sense of anything.

She suddenly reminds me of my mother. As she continues yelling, it's like watching acid drip from a battery with all the toxins leaking out. How did I not see this about her? I watched her so closely. The anger just starts burning away inside me and I have to think quickly.

"Yes, me," I reply. "You have no idea what I'm capable of. You shouldn't have lied to me, Sara. I really didn't want to have to hurt you."

Her expression suddenly changes to confusion. "What the hell are you going on about, Daniel? We haven't got time to mess about."

"I'm not messing about. I can't let you hurt Marie or John, and now I can't let you get away," I tell her without taking my eyes off her.

"Okay, you're scaring me a little now, Daniel, just stop. It's really not the time."

I can tell she doesn't know if I'm being serious or not. Her eyes are frantically searching mine for the truth, so I tell her about Tina.

"You remember how horrible she was to you that day, accusing you of lying to her? Rightly so, apparently. I threw her over that balcony, for you. I wish I hadn't now."

"You're saying that like it's no big deal. You can't have killed her, Daniel. Tell me you didn't, please," she pleads.

She looks scared now. I can see the panic in her eyes, like she's trying to work out her next move.

"I love you, Daniel," she says with tears in her eyes, like she knows this could be the end for her. I don't believe her and I don't trust her.

As she makes a move to get out of the car, I grab her scarf from the foot well and wrap it as tight as I can around her neck. My hands are shaking the whole time. She fights a lot longer than I expect her to.

So much for our lovely wedding. She's ruined everything, just like Helen did. I always seem to pick the wrong ones. They either turn out to be crazy or they think I am. Better I find out now though.

I place Sara's body back in the seat properly and somehow make my legs, which are like jelly, move to get out of the car. I wasn't nervous like this with Helen, maybe it's because this was more sudden and not planned. I get away as fast as I can. I can hear another vehicle stop in the background.

Sara must have thought Liam was responsible for Tina's death when the police said her fall from the balcony was suspicious. She never even suspected me. I feel bad now for killing her to protect Sara. Sara wasn't the one that needed protecting, Tina was. I hate when I get it wrong and I was so wrong about Sara. Maybe I'll take a break from women for a while. It never ends well. I leave Sara there in the car and hope that the police don't figure out too soon what's really happened here. I need time to get away.

I go to see Liam as soon as it's light. I hand over a vial of salt that I tell him I took from Sara before she died.

Liam is an idiot. He has no idea what it is and he trusts me. I do feel a little guilty. He tries to act like he's sorry about what happened to Sara but I can tell that he's not. When he hands that over to his buyer, I'll be long gone.

He's so wrapped up in selling this that he forgets to ask for the wristband back, just like I knew he would.

I make sure my pay is cleared before I leave.

36

Sara

Daniel tries to grab the wheel. *He's going to get us killed,* I think, before the car swerves off the road.

When I come round, the panic sets back in and I realise I have to find Marie and John.

I'm yelling at Daniel while also trying to calm the nausea that's rising in my stomach. I don't know if it's because maybe I got hurt in the accident. I haven't tried to move much yet.

I tell Daniel again we have to go back, while my head tries to regain stability from the spinning.

I snap and tell him about Liam and the danger I've put us in. I'm barely taking in anything he says until he says he can't let me leave.

He starts talking about Tina. I can't believe what I'm hearing.

"I killed her."

It wasn't Liam, it was my gentle Daniel. I'm yelling *no, no, no,* but I realise I'm just yelling it in my head. My whole body has frozen with fear and my voice won't work. What's going on? I can't absorb all this information, it's all wrong.

I look into this person's eyes, I say person because as hard as I try to search for Daniel in there, I don't see him anymore. A dangerous stranger is sitting there talking to me, one with eyes that are so cold I don't recognise them. He's just confessed to murdering someone. How do I get Daniel back? Can I even get him back?

"I love you," I'm finally able to say, which is true. I know my fate is sealed when he doesn't say it back.

I have to at least try to get away. I put up a worthless fight before everything fades to black in front of me.

37

Marie

We put the news on in the morning and watch as the reporter announces, "Preliminary reports suggest that the driver, a young woman, had been killed after the accident. This is now a murder investigation. Two men have been linked to the crime. They were seen in close proximity to the crime scene and are employees of a known criminal, Liam Edwards, who had some kind of work connection with the victim. He has yet to be questioned."

"Looks like Sara was caught up with the wrong people," I say to John. "I wonder if those guys are looking for Daniel too. Do you think we could be in danger?"

"I don't think so, those two guys will probably end up in jail along with that Liam guy they're looking for. We'll be fine."

"What a couple of weeks it's been," I say to John.

"It's definitely been interesting. Strange they haven't mentioned Daniel at all. Do you think he could be hiding out somewhere?" John asks.

"Maybe, we might never know."

As I say that I get a strange shiver, the kind you get when

they say someone just walked over your grave, or like you've just had a very narrow escape. It's like the one I had walking to the cafe that bizarre morning that I met them. It feels like a relief that they're out of our lives

38

Daniel

I decided to use the wristband to go back to my first year of college, to a time when I was happy. This was where I met Sara. I gave her my seat on the bus on the way to my classes that day. This time, I take an earlier bus. Yes, she'll still need to be dealt with but this time I have options. It won't have to be on the spur of the moment, unplanned. I'll come up with something that won't put me in the frame for it, preferably something where her body won't ever be found.

My dad is coming to visit me on the weekend. I went to visit him quickly this morning, before I left. I don't regret getting rid of my mother. I have a responsibility to get rid of the toxic people I come across. I'm just doing the world a favour.

This new beginning for me has so many possibilities. I can return as many times as I want, correcting mistakes. It's quite exciting really. I may look up a certain Lisa in the future, sounds like she was awful to Marie. I know she was just a kid but she's bound to grow up still carrying that selfish streak. I'm not a monster, though. I wouldn't hurt anyone who didn't deserve it. I'll watch her first from a distance and figure out what she's like now. I like people watching, it's always been a kind of hobby of mine.

I hope Marie and John have a good future together. I'll leave them alone to enjoy their lives. They're better off putting the whole Sara and me business behind them.

I will miss Sara. I really thought she was the one. I can still see her standing in front of that shop mirror with that beaming smile. It's a shame she had to go. It just goes to show how little you can really know someone. I think she did love me but realised it too late. I would never have been able to trust her again. The look in her eyes when I told her about Tina tells me I wouldn't have been forgiven. She would have gone straight to the police.

I know there's someone out there for me. I may pick a few of the wrong ones before I get to the right one but I don't have to rush now.

On my way to my first class I bump into Annie. She smiles and says hi. She seems like a nice girl.

"Do you want to get a coffee or something later?" I ask shyly.

"Yes, that sounds nice. I could meet you back here at half twelve, if that's okay for you?" she says with a genuine-looking smile.

"That's great, I'll see you then," I reply.

I have a good feeling about Annie. I can't help but smile to myself as I walk away.

***

My mother was awful to my father, she treated him like shit.

They were happy when I was a kid though. I remember them always taking me out to places and we always had a good time.

Then the arguments started when I was in my early teens.

My mother started sleeping around and kept shouting at my father over any little thing. He only had to be in the room sometimes to set her off. She had gone from a loving mother and wife to a bitch.

I used to hear my father crying in the nights while she was out with some other guy. She didn't even care anymore that he knew. He was drinking heavily then, but through everything he still always had time for me. I think he knew I felt abandoned too.

One night, while I was watching my dad drink himself into oblivion again, she phoned asking me to pick her up. Her date had left and she had no money to get home. She could barely speak, she was slurring her words. I knew she'd had too much to drink. I wasn't even old enough to pass my driving test but she didn't care.

"Just take the keys and come and get me. Do something useful for once in your life," she snapped at me.

So I did. I ended her cruelty that night.

She was passed out in the passenger's seat of the car. All I had to do was drive to the lake, move her into the driving seat, and steer the car in. I don't think my heart even raised a beat, I felt nothing. That is what she had reduced me to.

Everyone would assume she was drunk at the wheel. It wouldn't be a surprise to anyone, least of all my father.

My father still drank but he seemed more at peace now, not watching the door dreading when she would be coming home.

I wasn't a bit sorry. She deserved what she got. She ruined my father's life, and I missed the dad he used to be. I missed our family but I could never look at her the same way again. She didn't care about anyone but herself.

This is why I had to get rid of Sara. She would have eventually become just like her. I could see it starting in her eyes when she spoke to me in the car. That cold look, with no emotion. I want a good woman to have children with, not a copy of my mother. I have to look out for myself.

Helen was the same. She seemed so nice at first, but soon she started going for drinks after work all the time.

"I'm just trying to get to know my work colleagues," she would say in tears. She denied anything was going on when I asked her, but I saw that she was distracted. "They're just people that I work with," she would argue, but I could see it. All the signs were there, and she was getting more distant.

I may be slow at times picking up on the signals but I will find out eventually. Nobody can hide from me.

39

Rose (Marie's Mother, 1978)

I'm giving the teddy bear a wipe over with a damp cloth. You can never be too careful with second hand things, especially for kids. When I'm going over the back, I feel something hard inside. I check to see if there's a section there for batteries maybe, but no, it's definitely inside and there's no opening there. I carefully cut through a few of the stitches at the back, just enough to see inside. There's a small plastic container amongst the stuffing with some kind of powder inside.

I take it into the living room to show David.

"It has to be drugs," I tell him, still in shock at what I've found inside a child's toy.

"It does look like it. It can't be anything good, that's for sure, to be hidden away like that. I've an idea." He goes out the back and grabs a small shovel. "I'll bury it deep down so that nobody will ever find it."

I can't help but joke that David's garden comes first to his mind in most situations and I ask him will he be burying me there when I pass.

"I can just picture it now," I say. "'I'm sorry sir but your wife is no longer with us.' 'Okay I'll just go get my shovel,

I've always wanted a Rose garden.'" And we both laugh hysterically.

***

David

Rose starts to shush me after a while, she doesn't want Marie to hear us and come down yet.

"Just make sure it's right out of reach of anyone," she says. "I still can't believe someone would be stupid enough to hide drugs in a child's teddy bear."

"Well, they won't hurt anyone now, thanks to you Rose."

"What if someone comes looking for them? The teddy must've been on that stall by mistake," Rose says.

"If that's the case, they won't know you bought it," I reassure her, "and anyway, it's just a small amount, not enough to lose someone a great deal of money. Let's just forget we ever saw them."

"Okay, you're right. I shouldn't be afraid anyway, they should. I'm really mad about this."

"I would be afraid," David says with a giggle. "Now let's forget all about it and sew the teddy back up before Marie comes down from her bath. It's gone now."

Before we do that, Rose's favourite song, *Where Do You Go To, My Lovely?*, comes on the radio, so I serenade her around the garden. She tells me to stop being silly, but we carry on dancing.

40

Daniel's Father

I know Daniel killed his mother. He had that vague, distracted look about him, just like I did after the first time.

My wife was horrified when she came across the jewellery that I'd managed to hide away in the attic. She immediately recognised them from the news, they'd been on there often enough over the years. 'Trophies', they called them.

I came home and found her in the attic. She flinched when I went near her. There was no point in denying it now, she already knew. Her husband was a serial killer. I saw the life drain out of her right at that very moment. My former lovely wife was reduced to a person I no longer recognised . She couldn't look at me anymore without hatred in her eyes. She never spoke of it again or went to the police. It was like I broke her. She became hell bent on destroying me and ended up destroying herself in the process. I don't think she could forgive herself for not seeing it sooner.

We'd been married for ten years before we had Daniel. We thought having kids would never happen for us, so you can understand how happy Lucy was to finally have a child. But even Daniel couldn't make her smile anymore.

She distanced herself from me as much as she could, Daniel too. He always stood by me, and she couldn't bear it. The drink only helped a little. I didn't kill anyone else after that day. I can't speak to Daniel about it, though, he'd hate me forever. I made him kill his own mother.

My first time was long before Daniel was even born. Little did my wife Lucy know but she had already found one of my trophies back then, she just didn't know what it was.

From my first victim, I took an orange teddy bear from her dressing table. It had a little note attached to it with a guy's name and the following days date. I figured it was a present for someone, so maybe nobody would even know it was missing. I should have picked something smaller, but I wasn't thinking clearly. Everything was a blur that night.

When I got home, Lucy was already back and I didn't hide the teddy bear in time. When she asked what it was for, I told her I found it on the street on the way home and thought she could put it in the collection for the jumble sales she ran. She and her friends collected stuff all the time for charity and sent them off to all different places to be sold at different events, usually carnivals or jazz band competitions. At least nobody would discover who it belonged to now, just a random toy at a jumble sale. So I never had a trophy from my first time. That's when I decided on jewellery, it's easier to hide. Or so I thought.

It's still hard getting by without the drink to block everything out. I've relapsed a few times now, but Daniel helps me get back on my feet every time. When I'm sober, I can't ignore the guilt I feel for what I did to Lucy, but I try to stay sober for Daniel's sake. I destroyed our family, it's the least I can do.

I probably would've got caught had I not stopped after the sixteenth victim.

All I can do for Daniel now is be there for him when he

gets caught, which he will eventually.

41

Marie

We settle on the sofa to look through some of the photos we took on our phones from the days we went back. We were too tired last night.

We knew Sara and Daniel were lying about most stuff, why not about taking photos?

I'm glad we took the chance. I now have that lovely memory of my mam and dad dancing in the garden, there in colour photos and video on my phone. My mam in her lovely red dress and both of them laughing. I'll take this later to show her. I've got a feeling she might believe me now. John also has a photo of his Pepper bike because I'd never heard of them and he wanted to show me. He also got one of his sister with a coal bucket on her head. Of course he did.

We take a selfie on the sofa with Chewy on John's lap and me cwtching my new bright orange teddy bear that John surprised me with today. I won't be calling this one Amber, it'll get a new name.

I'll always remember the day I got Amber. My mam and dad were standing out in the garden, Mam still in her red dress. The top window was slightly open, as it always was in the summer. A gentle breeze weaved its way slowly into my bedroom. I could hear my mam and dad laughing outside, so I went over to the window.

"Just make sure it's right out of reach of anyone," I heard Mam say. "I still can't believe someone would be stupid enough to hide drugs in a child's teddy bear."

I watched my dad dig a small but deep hole in the garden, but he wasn't digging near the vegetables like he usually did.

I continued to watch, trying to understand what was happening. From what I could hear, it sounded like someone had hidden drugs in my new teddy bear and neither of them were happy about it. I felt a little scared, especially when Mam said, "I hope nobody comes looking for it", but that's not why I remember the day so well.

Dad told Mam she looked pretty in her red dress, and they danced around in the garden. The sun was just setting over the mountain that sat across from my bedroom window, giving off a reflection of orange hues across the sky and lighting up the garden, making it look magical.

Where Do You Go to, My Lovely? was playing on the radio. Mam was laughing and calling Dad silly. They looked so happy. That's why I always remember that evening, the two of them dancing around the garden, looking at each other like it was their first dance ever. It always makes me smile.

I'm disappointed that Sara and Daniel thought I was just some idiot that swallowed up their story. I knew what they wanted, but I wasn't going to tell them that or tell them what happened to what was inside Amber. What they were looking for wasn't there anymore.

I wanted to go back in time, and I knew John would want to as well. Plus, the money will be handy if we or our children ever need anything.

I am sorry about what happened to Sara. I'm guessing her boss wasn't happy with her, but she clearly knew what she was doing. I did, for a while, hope I was wrong. I'd started to like her and Daniel.

John knew all about it too. I'd told him years ago about one of the best memories I had of my mam and dad dancing in the garden that evening, but I'd forgotten about the rest of it until Sara and Daniel turned up at the café that day.

It all started coming back to me when I was relaxing in the bath that evening. As soon as I remembered it more clearly, I went back downstairs and told John all about it. We discussed it and decided to just use the opportunity to go back and not say anything. Why should we? They weren't honest with us.

We will never know how much Sara and Daniel knew, or what was inside the bear. We don't care.

I never told my mother that I overheard them in the garden that night. I think she would have just worried more about it.

***

Today is a brand-new day. We pack up a picnic basket, grab a couple of folding chairs, and load them up into our new VW transporter. We can venture further afield now and maybe even stay overnight somewhere. One of the kids will take care of Chewy. Each day can be a new adventure or discovery, just like when we were kids, but now we get to share them with each other.

I guess we never really knew Sara and Daniel that well. Who knows, maybe he killed her. We'll never really know what happened and we don't want to. As long as we keep quiet about everything we do know, we should be safe from him and anyone else involved.

I don't think my mother would have approved of Sara and Daniel. I can hear her now, 'psychos, the pair of them, you mark my words'.

We must have seemed like pushovers to Sara and Daniel. I

don't know if they really thought we were that naive and clueless, but I think they were the blind ones.

I do know that they should've known better than to underestimate a valleys girl.

Acknowledgements

I would like to thank my husband, Paul, for listening to me rant constantly while trying to write this. Also, for putting up with my indecisiveness about the cover and title, and asking your opinion about fifty times when I kept changing my mind. And, of course, for taking care of me always, especially this last year while I've been ill. Thank you for the Dr Martens idea. How could I not include them in the story after you constantly nagged me to?

To my daughter, and brilliant editor, Jodie Leigh Evans, for all the hardwork you put in, even though you're always incredibly busy and trying to search for time to write your own book, which I know will be amazing.

This book is fictional and started out as a lighthearted, time-travelling story that eventually turned into a thriller. I've read so many good thrillers by amazing authors. That's what gave me the inspiration to keep going in that direction.

The book is set in the beautiful Welsh valleys, where I grew up and where I wrote this book.

Printed in Great Britain
by Amazon